Choose your dream destination to say "I Do"!

Applegate Ranch, Montana:
Get your lasso at the ready for rugged rancher Dillon in
RODEO BRIDE by Myrna Mackenzie

Loire Valley, France:
You don't need a magic wand for a fairy tale in France,
with handsome château owner Alex as your host!
**CINDERELLA ON HIS DOORSTEP
by Rebecca Winters**

Principality of Carvainia, Mediterranean:
Step into Aleks's turreted castle
and you'll feel like a princess!
**HER PRINCE'S SECRET SON
by Linda Goodnight**

Manhattan, New York:
Stroll down Fifth Avenue
on the arm of self-made millionaire Houston.
**RESCUED IN A WEDDING DRESS
by Cara Colter**

Naples, Italy:
The majesty of Mount Vesuvius and dangerously
dashing Dante will make your senses erupt!
**ACCIDENTALLY EXPECTING!
by Lucy Gordon**

Sydney, Australia:
Hotshot TV producer Dan is on the lookout
for someone to star in his life....
**LIGHTS, CAMERA...KISS THE BOSS
by Nikki Logan**

Dear Reader,

One of the greatest things about writing a story is meeting the characters and getting to know them. I start out with a vague idea of who they are, but by the end of the book they've become real, warm, caring human beings. Here are some things I learned about Colleen and Dillon as the story unfolded.

Colleen is a woman who:

Is a former champion barrel racer

Is a Montana rancher

Is strong and willing to go to bat for those she loves

Loves the color red and has a great pair of red cowgirl boots

Can't have children, even though she was born to be a mother

Has been mistreated by those who should have loved her

Catches fire whenever Dillon is around, even though she shouldn't!

Dillon is a man who:

Is a millionaire who owns his own engineering firm in Chicago

Has returned from battle wounded

Is a protector of the weak

Never knew he wanted children, but will move heaven and earth to be with his son

Loves fast, sleek cars

Has some dark moments in his past that he would rather not remember

A tough lady rancher tied to the land, and a millionaire Chicago entrepreneur? I didn't know how that would ever work out, but I knew that love would find a way!

Best wishes

Myrna Mackenzie

MYRNA MACKENZIE

Rodeo Bride

HARLEQUIN®

TORONTO • NEW YORK • LONDON
AMSTERDAM • PARIS • SYDNEY • HAMBURG
STOCKHOLM • ATHENS • TOKYO • MILAN • MADRID
PRAGUE • WARSAW • BUDAPEST • AUCKLAND

PLEASE RECYCLE
THIS PRODUCT IS RECYCLABLE

Recycling programs
for this product may
not exist in your area.

ISBN-13: 978-0-373-74006-2

RODEO BRIDE

First North American Publication 2010.

Copyright © 2009 by Myrna Topol.

www.eHarlequin.com

Printed in U.S.A.

Myrna Mackenzie grew up not having a clue what she wanted to be (she hadn't been born a princess, the one job she thought she might like because of the steady flow of pretty dresses and crowns), but she knew that she loved stories and happy endings, so falling into life as a romance writer was pretty much inevitable. An award-winning author with more than thirty-five novels written, Myrna was born in a small town in Dunklin County, Missouri, grew up just outside Chicago and now divides her time between two lakes in Chicago and Wisconsin, both very different and both very beautiful. She adores the Internet (which still seems magical after all these years), loves coffee, hiking, "attempting" gardening (without much success), cooking and knitting. Readers (and other potential gardeners, cooks, knitters, writers, etc.) can visit Myrna online at www.myrnamackenzie.com or write to her at P.O. Box 225, La Grange, IL 60525.

Ranching. It sounds like a romantic profession, rife with history and symbolism. But what's it really all about? What *is* a typical day on a ranch like, anyway?

That's a good question, but the answer may well be…there isn't a typical day. Ranching is a year-round job with no set hours and no time off. Cattle and horses and other animals don't cooperate with a nine-to-five schedule, the tasks change with the seasons and nature doesn't care if the weather is bad. Jobs must get done, animals have to be fed and cared for and tended to when they're sick.

So what are some of the tasks a cowboy (or cowgirl) does over the course of a year? There's a range, a daunting variety. In the winter, cows must be fed on a daily basis. Repairs must be made to equipment on an ongoing basis. Fences and buildings must be repaired. Snow has to be plowed and firewood chopped. Whew! It sounds like an awful lot of work, and it is, but…life isn't all work.

Occasionally the rancher gets into town or there's a picnic or a rodeo or a wedding or other gathering. Friends and neighbors and other ranchers come out to help with the branding or the haying (with a feast, of course).

Despite the never-ending work and the fickleness of nature that sends blizzards, bitter temperatures, drought or heavy rains into play to make the tasks more difficult, there are those who would have it no other way, who would prefer no other job and who love this profession that keeps them close to the land and to the rhythms of nature.

In the end it's not about the hat. It's about the lifestyle. It's all about the cowboy and his relationship to the land and the animals he (or she) loves.

CHAPTER ONE

DILLON FARRADAY was coming. "This morning," Colleen Applegate whispered, staring out the window at the long drive leading from her ranch to the rest of the world. And the reason he was coming was going to tear her heart apart, she thought, glancing down at the baby monitor, her lifeline to the child she'd grown to love as her own.

She'd never actually met the man, but what she knew worried her. He was drop-dead handsome, rich and, therefore, probably used to getting his way. He was from Chicago and might frown on Montana ranch life. Moreover, he was a soldier, used to harsh ways, and Colleen knew all about harsh men. This one had been injured in battle six months ago, so he might not be in the best of humor. All of that information was public, readily available on the Internet.

Beyond that, however, things got murkier. Dillon was recently divorced from Lisa, a former local who had gone to school with Colleen, and three months ago Lisa had shown up at Colleen's door with her new baby. "I can't do this," she'd told Colleen, "but you're perfect with babies, and you've always wanted one. Take care of him, please, for now."

Colleen had wanted to say no, but a baby had been involved. She'd reluctantly agreed to keep Toby safe.

"By the way," Lisa had said, before she left, "I sent a note to Dillon at the hospital where he's laid up, so he knows about the baby's existence. He might or might not want to see Toby someday, but…the baby might not be his. Biologically, that is."

Then Lisa had run, so that small cryptic bit of information was almost all that Colleen knew. Except for one more thing. That question about whether or not Dillon might want to see the baby? It was no longer a question.

In a brief, terse telephone conversation yesterday he had introduced himself, said that he'd been released from the hospital and indicated one thing more: he was coming to Montana and he expected Colleen to docilely hand sweet little Toby over.

There was only one problem there. Dillon Farraday might have a legal claim, but Colleen had never been a docile woman.

Moreover, she had questions, and she intended to get good solid answers before she simply handed over an innocent baby, one she loved, to anyone, especially to a man she didn't know or trust.

Dillon parked his black Ferrari in front of the long, low log house. The beauty of the mountains was behind him, but other than this lopsided house and the outbuildings, there were no signs of civilization for miles around. Why on earth had Lisa left the baby here? And why had she waited so long to let him know of the child's existence?

The same questions—and possible answers—had been swirling through his head for weeks, but he had spent a lifetime learning to bide his time, to think things through to their logical conclusion and then to act when the time was right. His marriage to Lisa had seemed to follow the same pattern, but in reality it had been the one glaring exception and an obvious mistake. But now that he was capable of walking a reasonable distance, driving a reasonable distance, the time was definitely right for lots of things he hadn't been able to take care of before.

He would have his answers…and his son. Colleen Applegate couldn't legally deny him, and she probably knew that. She hadn't sounded happy to hear from him when he'd called yesterday.

Too bad. She could have touched base with him anytime during the past three months and she hadn't bothered to do that, so her opinions didn't matter. All that mattered about Colleen Applegate was that she had his child.

Dillon pulled himself from the car, took the darned cane he was still forced to use and approached the house that appeared to have been put together haphazardly, like a child using two different sets of blocks that didn't fit together. There were two front steps. Sloping steps. Those would be a problem. He didn't like anyone seeing him struggle, so when the door opened and a woman stepped out onto the slanted porch, he stayed where he was.

"Ms. Applegate?" he asked.

"You're half an hour early," she said with a nod.

Somehow Dillon managed to conceal his surprise at her appearance. Lisa had always been friends with women who were a lot like herself: model-thin and petite with skillfully made-up faces and expensive clothing that accentuated their willowy figures. Colleen Applegate was tall and curvy with messy, riotous blond curls and little if any makeup. She was dressed in a red T-shirt, jeans and boots. There were no signs of vanity about her. No smile, either, and her comment clearly indicated irritation.

For some reason that made him want to smile. Maybe because of the interest factor. He'd been raised to command, and people had been tiptoeing around him all his adult life. His employees, his soldiers, apparently even his ex-wife. But this woman wasn't tiptoeing. Not even slightly.

"Traffic was light," he said with a smile and a shrug.

She looked instantly wary. He supposed he could understand why. This situation had to be uncomfortable for her at best. If she'd grown attached to the baby, it would be worse than that. He noted that she had brown eyes…expressive eyes that signaled a woman who had trouble hiding her thoughts. "You know why I'm here," he said.

"You made that clear yesterday."

Dillon studied those pretty brown eyes. He had seen a lot of pain in the past year, his own physical pain the least of it. This woman was in pain.

He closed his eyes and tried to pretend she was the enemy. No use. *Damn Lisa for bringing another person into this. If she'd wanted to punish him for neglecting her when he traveled for work and went to war, that was fine, but a child? This woman who was clearly emotionally affected by all this?*

He looked at Colleen. "I want my child." His voice was low, quiet, a bit raspy. "Can you blame me?"

She bit her lip and shook her head. Those eyes looked even sadder. "No." The word was barely a whisper. "Come in. He's sleeping."

"Just like that? Don't you want proof that I am who I am? Identification?"

Something close to a smile lifted her lips. "You're a millionaire and a war hero, Mr. Farraday. That makes you easy to find on the Internet. I don't actually need proof that you're who you say you are."

He nodded.

"But I'll look at your identification. To verify your address and any other particulars I might not have thought of. I want all of this done right. Every *i* dotted and every *t* crossed. I have questions. Lots of them, but none of them have to do with a photo ID."

"What kinds of questions are they, then?"

"Whether you'll be a good father, whether Toby will get everything he needs."

The obvious, automatic answer would have been to say that Toby would be given all that money could buy, but Dillon knew all too well that money was never enough. His upbringing and his failed marriage were proof of that. Colleen Applegate was right on the money with her qualms. He couldn't even argue with her.

And despite her invitation to come inside, she was still standing in front of the door as if to guard his son from him.

"I intend to be a good father," he said, and prayed that he could live up to his intentions. Children were fragile in so many ways.

Colleen still didn't budge.

"I meant that," he said.

"I'm not doubting your word, but—"

"But you don't know me," he suggested. "You know my public history, but you don't know what kind of man I really am. Is that it?"

She hesitated. "Something like that. I don't mean to be rude, but I've gotten used to worrying about Toby. I have to live with myself after I turn him over to you, and he's still so little."

"Understood," Dillon said, even as a small streak of admiration for Colleen Applegate's determination to guard his child crept in.

She needed reassurance. He needed his child. The fact that so much time had already passed, that he'd missed so much...

Anger at these circumstances shot straight through Dillon. Disregarding his appearance and his own embarrassment at his weakness, he struggled up onto the porch and moved to within a foot of Colleen, towering over her despite her height.

"I understand your reticence," he assured her. "I see your point. Here's mine. Toby *is* my son. And while I have no experience whatsoever at being a father, I intend to do everything in my power to make sure Toby is happy."

Dillon held her gaze. He noted the small flutter of her pulse at her throat. He knew that his height and stoic demeanor often intimidated people, but while Colleen was noticeably nervous, she was still standing tall and proud. However reluctant he was to give ground to this woman, he had to admire her for not wilting before his anger. Still, the worried look in her eyes eased. Just a bit.

"He's sleeping," she reminded him, as if she had to get the last word in.

He fought not to smile. "I won't wake him."

Colleen sighed. "He's a light sleeper, but his naptime is almost over, anyway. Come inside." She finally turned and opened the door, leading him into the house.

There was something about the way she moved that immediately attracted his attention. It wasn't a sway, the kind of thing that other men reacted to. It was both less and more. Tall and long-legged, she moved with confidence, sleekly and quietly making her way through the house.

Instantly, his male antennae went on alert. The attraction was surprisingly intense. Also wrong, given the situation. Obviously his months in a military hospital out of the mainstream were having an effect.

That was unacceptable. He was here for one reason only, to find his child. And even if he weren't, he'd been betrayed by women too many times to jump in blindly again. A man who had been betrayed by his mother, his first love and his wife should have learned his lesson by now.

I have, he thought. Women were out, at least in any meaningful way.

So he concentrated on being as silent as Colleen, trying not to knock his cane against anything. The baby was asleep in the depths of this rambling house. This very old, and in need of repairs and paint, rambling house, Dillon noted, as Colleen came to a stop outside a door.

"Here," she whispered, touching her finger to her lips.

Dillon came up close behind her. The light soap scent of her filled his nostrils. He ignored his own body's reaction and stared into a room unlike the others he'd passed through. The walls were a robin's egg blue. Clouds and stars and moons were stenciled on a border that circled the room just below the ceiling. A sturdy white crib with a mobile of dancing horses hanging above it sat in the corner, and in the crib lay a chubby little child in a pale yellow shirt and diaper, his skin rosy and pink, his fingers and toes unbelievably tiny.

Toby Farraday, Dillon thought. His child. His heir. He had had many people in his life, but none, not even his parents, certainly not his wife, who had truly been his.

He glanced down at Colleen, who, despite the fact that she had been living with Toby for months, seemed totally entranced by the sight, too. She glanced up at Dillon. "He's beautiful, isn't he?" she whispered.

Her voice was soft and feminine and the way she

had looked at the baby, the fact that they all seemed to be closed up in this cozy, warm, safe cocoon...

Was an illusion, Dillon knew. Safety and security of that type weren't real. He couldn't afford to fall into that kind of thinking, not now when he had someone other than himself he was responsible for. Reality was key to avoiding disillusionment for his son...and for himself.

"Is that one of your questions?" he asked.

She blinked. "Pardon me?"

"You told me you had many questions. Is asking me if my son is beautiful a test? If I should say no..."

Anger flashed in her eyes. "Then you'd be a liar."

"Ah, so it was a test," he said, his tone teasing. "Yes, he's beautiful, Ms. Applegate."

She grimaced. "No one calls me that."

He had the distinct impression that the last time someone had called her that, it hadn't been a pleasant experience.

"Then yes, he's beautiful, Colleen. And I'm not lying."

"Good. I'm glad you feel that way because..." Those deep brown eyes filled with concern again.

"What?"

"I hate to even bring this up...but before I completely turn him over to you, there's something that has to be asked. There's a potential problem."

Still she hesitated. He was pretty sure he knew why. Given the fact that there was nothing in the public history she had read that could have caused her to worry, there could be only one thing remaining that was making her this uncomfortable.

"Ask," he demanded, the single word clipped and cold.

Colleen took a deep, visible breath and looked right into his eyes.

"What if Lisa…there might be a chance…I wouldn't ordinarily even bring up something so painful and so…not my business, but as I mentioned, I have to make sure Toby's okay, and…what if he isn't your biological son?"

Anger pulsed through Dillon even as he told himself that her question was a valid one for a woman who saw herself as the sole protector of an innocent baby.

"If you think I haven't heard that my wife had…intimate friends even before we divorced, then you're wrong. If you're suggesting that I would take out my displeasure on a baby, then you haven't really done your research on me after all and you haven't been listening to me. And if you think for one second that this changes things, then let me tell you that it doesn't. Whether Toby is my biological son or not, he's legally mine. I was married to Lisa when he was conceived, and the law is clear on my claim to him."

His words and tone would have cowed most people. But Colleen didn't drop her gaze even one bit. She was, he conceded, acting like the proverbial mother bear, even if Toby wasn't hers.

"I'm not the type of guy who would let that make a difference. I no longer have a wife, so what Lisa did or didn't do doesn't matter to me. What I have is a son. He's not responsible for his parentage. No one ever is." Thank goodness.

Colleen visibly relaxed. "Thank you. Some men wouldn't feel that way."

"I'm not those men." His last words may have been uttered a bit too loudly. Toby made a small, unhappy whimpering sound.

Faster than light, quieter than the dawn, Colleen was across the room. She reached down and gently stroked the baby's arm. "Shh, you're safe, sweetheart," she whispered. "I'm here. No one will hurt you."

Almost instantly, the baby calmed. He pulled one fist up to his mouth and began to suck his thumb. He slept, his long lashes fluttering back down over those pale, pretty cheeks. Colleen gazed down at the baby with what looked like true affection. Had any of his nannies ever looked like that when he was growing up? Dillon wondered. No, some of them had been decent, but not even close to being that involved. He hadn't expected them to, hadn't even known it was possible. Still, this was…nice, even though her attachment to the baby was clearly going to be a problem.

Colleen looked up into Dillon's eyes, that naked pain evident again. Dillon wanted to look away. He forced himself not to.

She stood straight and tall, proudly defying him while she still could. For an Amazon she didn't look even slightly out of place in this room full of small things. He noted the stuffed animals in a sun-yellow crate, the changing table with diapers and lotions, the piles of baby clothes on top of a child-sized dresser, the toys and books. A night-light shaped like a lamb. Now, he remembered that he'd passed a stroller on the way in, a bright blue playpen in the living room. Where had all these things come from?

As if she'd read his mind, she moved toward him. "We need to talk," she said.

"My thoughts exactly."

"We have about thirty minutes before Toby wakes up in earnest. He's like clockwork and then he'll want to be fed." She ushered Dillon toward the living room, where she perched on a chair that had a lot more years on it than anything in the nursery. Dillon sat down on a tired old sofa.

With the playpen taking up a lot of the space, the room seemed small, tight, not quite big enough for two adults. Dillon looked at Colleen, and now, without the foil of Toby to concentrate on, she looked nervous, rubbing her palms over her jeans.

Dillon's gaze followed her hands down her legs. He ordered himself to think of the business at hand, not what Colleen Applegate's long legs looked like when they weren't encased in denim. There were important issues to deal with here. "Did Lisa give you money to take care of Toby?"

"Why would you think that?"

"Babies cost money. They take time."

"I haven't even had any contact with her since the day she dropped him here. He was only a week old. She didn't want him. I didn't even think of asking for payment. He was a baby with no one to love him."

"But you've obviously spent a fair amount of money. You'll be compensated."

She glared at him. "I don't want it. That would be like selling him." Those strong, sturdy hands were opening and closing now.

"All right. I won't insult you by offering again. Just tell me this. Why you? I'd never even heard of you before. Lisa never spoke of you. Were you good friends?"

Colleen shook her head, those messy curls brushing her cheeks. "We grew up in the same town and we went to school together, but no, we weren't friends at all. As for why, she seemed frantic, trapped and, well, this is a small town and everyone here knows me. It's no secret that I've always wanted children, but..."

"But you don't have any."

"No. I don't." It was clear that there was more to this part of the story than she was saying, but Dillon had no right to ask more. She had given him a valid answer.

"Lisa said that she couldn't be a mother to Toby," Colleen continued, "and she didn't say much more. She didn't stay long, and she seemed worried at what your reaction was going to be, as if she wanted to be gone before you got here."

"Which is why you have a number of questions of your own," he said.

"Partly, yes."

"Those questions you were asking earlier…you think I abused my wife or that I would once I knew that she had cheated on me?"

"I don't know you. I know there are men who can be abusive, with or without a reason. And even when abuse doesn't involve hitting it can be brutal and harmful." Something about the tone of her voice, the way she looked away when all along she'd been facing him head-on, led Dillon to believe that Colleen had had personal experience of such men. Something shifted inside him. Anger at his own kind filled him.

"I'm not a perfect man, Colleen, but I've never intentionally harmed a woman or a child, and I wouldn't."

She studied him as if trying to read his mind to see if he spoke the truth. Her eyes were dark and unhappy but she sucked in her lip, blinked and gave a hard nod. "Okay," she whispered. "I mean, I don't have a choice do I, but…"

Suddenly she leaned forward and opened a drawer on the end table next to the chair. She pulled out a sheaf of papers. Pages and pages of papers.

"These are things you need to know. Routines. Details on what went on during his first few months. His preferences, his quirks, his fears. Medical things. He was jaundiced when Lisa brought him here, and until recently, he was colicky, but if I wrapped him up tight in a blanket and rocked with him, eventually he would go to sleep. He takes a nap in the morning and one in the afternoon and…who will do all these things?" she asked suddenly. Then just as quickly she shook her head. "Forget I asked that. You're a wealthy man. You'll hire some…some nurse or something."

Someone who doesn't love him yet, she meant to say. Dillon was sure of that.

Gently, he took the stack of papers from Colleen. There were all kinds of notes. A description of Toby's first smile, his first laugh, which was just last week. His feeding schedule. More.

"You're right. I'm a wealthy man. I can hire a nurse." Just the way his parents had. A whole series of nurses and nannies who had come and gone. He didn't want that for his child.

"You could teach me what to do." The words just popped right out of nowhere. Dillon had no clue why he'd even said the words, but…

"I could take care of him," he added.

As if she wasn't even thinking, Colleen suddenly reached across and touched his hand. "That's incredibly sweet."

Dillon wanted to laugh. Sort of. "Have you looked at me, Colleen? No one on earth, least of all the people in my business or the men under my command, have ever called me sweet."

"I know." She looked down at where her hand lay on his, as if she regretted the move but didn't know how to take it back. "I didn't mean it quite the way it sounded. What I meant was, you don't have a clue what you're saying. Despite all your accomplishments, taking care of a baby is different from anything on earth you've ever done."

"I suspect that it is. So show me, Colleen."

"Now?"

"I've been away from my business for a long time. There are people I trust in charge, and they won't mind waiting for me a little longer. I have time for you to teach me."

Colleen worked hard at controlling her breathing. Dillon Farraday's hand was warm and strong and very masculine beneath her own. Not that she had any business noticing. Quickly, she pulled away.

"I don't feel comfortable having a man in my house."

Strange man. She should have said strange man. But she had meant what she said. She didn't want *any* man here. This whole house was her haven, her shelter, her barrier.

"You have other buildings. I could rent one."

For the first time she allowed herself to smile. "Some of them have animals in them, some have tools. You aren't exactly the type to bunk with the hired hands I employ."

"Don't judge a man by his looks, Colleen."

No, she never did. Looks could deceive. "I won't."

"Good. Then you'll let me stay here a few days? You'll train me in the basics so I can be a good father to Toby?"

"What will you do when you go back to Chicago? You'll still need someone."

"What do you do when you have to work around the ranch?"

"I bundle him up and take him with me or I find people I trust implicitly to help."

"Then I'll do that. Colleen?"

She looked straight into those ice-blue eyes and her heart began to pound fast. He was the most gorgeous, intimidating man she'd ever met. Not in the usual sense of the word. It wasn't that she thought he'd physically harm her, but something far different. He was the kind of man who could hurt her emotionally, and she was pretty sure that it wasn't just because he would take Toby. The smartest thing to do would be to run, to say no, and yet…

"You'll give me warning before you take him away?" she asked, trying to adjust to the sudden shift in plans.

She should be jumping at this, latching on to it. Dillon wanted to learn how to be a good father. That was a good thing, the best thing for Toby, and she would at least have a bit more time with the baby.

And with the man.

Colleen shoved that thought away. She hoped her face wasn't flaming. In the past, *her* past, well, a woman like her could easily look pathetic when she was attracted to a man, especially a man who was totally out of bounds.

"Will you let me stay?" he repeated. "Will you tutor me until I've got everything down pat and until Toby and I feel comfortable together?"

"You know I can't say no to that."

He smiled at her, and heat rushed through her. "Then say yes, Colleen."

She didn't even remember saying the word. She felt faint and sick and nervous, as if her body was not her own. But she must have said yes, because Dillon had gone outside and he was pulling a suitcase from his car.

A man was going to be staying with her here at the Applegate Ranch. She wondered what he would say when he discovered that all her employees were women.

CHAPTER TWO

MAYBE he should have stayed inside and read all that paperwork that Colleen had for him to pore over, but the enormity of what he was doing had finally hit, and Dillon needed a few minutes to regroup, so he stood on the porch leaning on the crooked railing as he looked out across the land. He'd spent a lifetime learning to control his emotions. Those lessons had served him well in business, and this past year with all that had happened, the merits of guarding his reactions had hit even harder.

But Colleen Applegate's passionate loyalty to his son had been unexpected. It had caught him off guard, which was most likely why he had made that uncharacteristically impetuous declaration that he wanted her to give him parenting lessons. He was already regretting that decision and yet, she was right. He didn't know a damn thing about caring for a baby and he wasn't about to let just anyone take over that task.

He swore beneath his breath. "What a mess."

The door opened behind him and when he turned to look at Colleen the expression on her face told him that she had, most likely, heard his last comment. Her chin was raised in defiance, and a trace of guilt slipped through Dillon. None of this, after all, was her fault.

"I apologize for the way that sounded."

All the defiance slipped away from her. "I doubt this was what you had anticipated when you thought about having children."

"I hadn't actually thought about it too much."

She studied him. "You didn't want a child?"

It hadn't been that so much. "I felt…unqualified. Still do. But he's here, and just because I hadn't anticipated him doesn't mean I don't want him. He's never going to feel as if his birth was a mistake, so don't even think that I'm heading down that path. I'm taking this job seriously."

"Job?"

"Dad."

Colleen gave a curt nod. "Okay, Dad. Let's get you settled. Then we'll get right to the father lessons."

Dillon saw now that she had a bundle of quilts in her arms. He reached out and started to take them from her but she shook her head.

"I can carry a few blankets," she said.

"I'm sure you can. You run a ranch. You tend to

my son. You have employees. But just because you can doesn't mean you should. I'm not a guest and I'm sure having me living here is an imposition that wasn't remotely in your plans for this week. If you won't let me compensate you for Toby's care, at least let me pull my weight." *Take back some of the control you've lost these past months,* he told himself. He'd grown up having no input into his parents' decision to farm him out to disinterested keepers. As a child, his quest for affection had only resulted in a roller-coaster ride of brief bouts of interest followed by long periods of apathy from both his parents and the people they hired to keep him fed, occupied and out of their way.

So, when he'd grown up, he'd turned to something ever dependable: logic and control. The precise environment of engineering never failed him. The reliability of being able to predict and control outcomes, and the measured skills involved in running a company and commanding troops, had been a perfect fit…until the events of the last year had blindsided him.

That time was over. He was not a man given to highs and lows and he'd made a mistake choosing someone as volatile as Lisa. Somehow, he'd missed who and what she was, just as the soldier walking ahead of him hadn't seen that land mine that had taken his life and injured Dillon. But, from now on, Dillon was putting the lid back on his emotions and regaining control of his life in even the most basic ways. He tugged on the quilts.

To his surprise, Colleen didn't let go. "This visit wasn't in your plans, either, I'm sure. And just so you know, so that there won't be too many surprises, ranch life's difficult," she countered. To her credit, she didn't glance at his leg, though he knew that was at least part of what she was referring to.

Dillon had a feeling that Colleen was one of those surprises. Was the woman really worrying about the welfare of the man who'd come to take the baby she clearly coveted?

"I'll let you know if it gets to be too much."

A small smile lifted her lips. "Somehow I doubt you would admit any such thing. You're an infuriatingly determined man, Mr. Farraday, but all right." She turned over the quilts.

He smiled slightly at her tone, but he didn't apologize. "Just Dillon will do. If you'll show me where I'm staying while I'm here, I'll get settled so that we can get right down to that crash course in fatherhood."

She hesitated. And hesitated some more. "The bunkhouse is occupied."

"And you don't feel comfortable having a man in your house," he remembered.

She looked uneasy. "I know that seems silly when I'm an independent woman who's been running a ranch for years, but—"

Dillon raised one hand to silence her. "You don't have to apologize or explain anything to me, Colleen. It doesn't sound silly. You're careful. That's good." Although he could tell from her expression that her concerns went deeper than simply being careful. Not his business. Nothing he needed to know about.

"Still, you're here to learn about taking care of Toby. You'll want to be near when he wakes up in the middle of the night. I have an enclosed back porch, and at this time of year you won't need heat. You won't have to worry about anyone intruding on you there. There's a door separating it from the house and a sleeper sofa that's…I'm sorry, I can't lie. It's *almost* comfortable."

Dillon wanted to smile, but she was clearly a bit embarrassed at her refusal to let him all the way inside her house. "I've been a soldier, Colleen. I've slept in the mud from time to time, and I'm used to less than comfortable circumstances, so I'm sure I'll be fine sleeping on the porch."

"Is he really staying?" a voice rang out. Dillon turned to see a big iron-haired woman making her way across the grass toward the house. "Gretchen said you called and told her that he was, but I didn't believe her. It's been a long time since we had a fine-looking man visiting the Applegate," the woman told Dillon.

Dillon glanced from a suddenly pink-faced

Colleen to the older woman. Colleen raised her chin and drew herself up.

"Millie, this is Dillon Farraday. He's—"

"Toby's father," the woman said. "Yes, I know."

"Millie is my right-hand woman," Colleen explained.

"She means that I cook, I clean, I mend and I take care of Toby when she has other duties to tend to," the woman said. She shoved out one large hand. "I can handle all the jobs that a man can handle, too, but…I miss having a man about the place. It's been a long time since I heard a deep voice around here."

Dillon shook her strong, weathered hand. "I thought Colleen said that she had other workers. Ranch hands. I assumed—"

Colleen sighed. "Millie, go get them. They must be in from their chores by now, anyway."

Without another word, Millie whipped out a cell phone, punched a few keys and just said, "Yes, now."

Immediately, Dillon heard female voices in the distance. He looked up to see two twentysomething women exit a building that had to be the bunkhouse. They headed toward the house.

"Wow, Mil, he's gorgeous. In a kind of rugged way," Dillon heard coming through the phone before Colleen reached over, plucked the phone from Millie and clicked it shut.

"I could have done that much," Colleen told her right-hand woman.

Millie shrugged. "Made more sense than running all the way back to the bunkhouse."

"Dillon might have needed some time to prepare himself," Colleen said. She stepped in front of him as if to protect him when the duo drew closer. He countered and moved to her side.

"Gretchen and Julie, this is Mr. Farraday," Colleen said. "He'll be with us for at least a few days. I'm pretty sure he doesn't bite, so show him what he needs to know if he asks. All right?"

"Of course. Will he be eating with us?" one of them asked.

"I normally eat in the bunkhouse," Colleen explained to Dillon. "It's just easier for Millie if we're all in one place, and the bunkhouse kitchen is newer and roomier. But for now," she said, turning toward the women, "I think Dillon might prefer it at the house with Toby. They're just getting to know each other."

Disappointment registered on at least one of the faces. Then the girls smiled and waved goodbye as they went back to the bunkhouse.

"I'll bring the food over soon," Millie said as she followed the girls.

Silence set in.

"I suppose you're wondering why I have only women working here."

He was. "I suppose you have your reasons and that they're none of my business. If you think I'm going to offer criticism, you're dead wrong. Some of the best soldiers I ever met were women and there are a number of fine female engineers working for my engineering firm. Besides, even though I don't know anything about ranching, your ranch looks as if it's in pretty good shape." In fact, the ranch looked significantly better than the house. Clearly, she was pumping her profits back into the business.

"Gretchen and Julie are young, they're strong, they're knowledgeable and they need this ranch to succeed as much as I do, so they put their all into it," Colleen said. "This is their home. They belong here."

And he didn't, Dillon knew. He and his shiny expensive car didn't belong here, but this was where he was going to begin again.

"Thank you for letting me stay and I'll tell the women thank-you when I see them again. I've already disrupted their routines by having you switch the meal. We don't have to do that."

She studied him carefully with those dark, serious eyes. "No, I think we do. Toby needs to get used to you being the one he focuses on. It will be easier for him if there aren't too many other distracting faces around at mealtimes. Not that he really eats meals exactly, but I make sure he's with us at the table. Being together at mealtime is important to a family."

He wouldn't know about that. His family had not been anything like a real family. "Is this my first lesson?" he asked with a smile.

He had clearly caught her by surprise with that question, and Colleen's cheeks pinked up again. Some women looked less attractive when they were flustered, but not this woman. When she took a long, deep breath, drew herself up to her full, impressive height and opened her mouth slightly as if choosing her words carefully, there was something utterly fascinating about her. As if she was concentrating all of her being into choosing those words. A sliver of heat slipped through Dillon... which wouldn't do at all.

Colleen shook her head, her curls brushing her shoulders. "I'm afraid I get carried away sometimes. The girls—the women, I mean—have been working here a couple of years, and since Julie is only twenty and Gretchen is twenty-three, a full five years younger than me, I guess I've gotten too used to doing that prim schoolteacher thing. Bad habit. I didn't mean to lecture, so no, that wasn't your first lesson."

Prim schoolteacher? Dillon couldn't help thinking that with Colleen's generous curves, *prim* was the last word that came to mind.

A strange, small sound suddenly filled the air. Automatically Colleen and Dillon both glanced down at her baby monitor.

It was the first time Dillon had heard his child's voice. "He's crying," Dillon said with wonder.

"Yes. And *that's* going to be your first lesson." Colleen held the door open. "You're going to hold your son," she said as Dillon brushed past her. The combination of her low, husky voice and the prospect of finally meeting his child face-to-face nearly made Dillon's knees buckle.

He'd faced disasters in his life, business barons and scenes in battle he'd prefer to forget. He had been suited to what he'd face in business and in battle. He had been trained and at least partially prepared for them. Nothing, he thought, had prepared him for the responsibility of molding a life that was so young and fragile.

He really was going to be dependent on Colleen, this woman he found far too intriguing. Bad move. He didn't do intriguing anymore, so somehow he had to learn all she could teach him as quickly as possible. Once he and Toby were on their own, they could sort everything else out and forget that this woman had ever been a part of their lives.

Everything about Dillon was too big, Colleen thought as she led him back to Toby's room. He was tall, his shoulders were broad, his hands were big with long fingers, his legs were long and well-muscled. Even with the limp, he seemed powerful and strong and she felt small. She never, ever felt small. That had been her mother, her charming, petite, pretty and utterly helpless mother, who had not passed along her genes to gawky, awkward, big-boned Colleen.

All of her life she'd wanted to be small. And now? Now, with Dillon behind her, dwarfing her, she just felt vulnerable. More awkward and self-conscious than ever. As if she'd just now realized that she was a woman. And all because Dillon, with that warrior's body of his, was most definitely a man.

"This way," she said, feeling instantly stupid.

Dillon chuckled, and Colleen felt her neck growing warm. "You're right. I guess I didn't need to direct you. You've been in here before," she conceded.

"And then there's the crying," he said dryly.

She couldn't help herself then. She laughed, too. "Your son does have a good set of lungs."

"Does he...does he cry often?"

She stopped, turned, and nearly ended up right against Dillon. Close, too close to that muscled chest. Colleen tipped her head up. She *never* tipped her head up to a man. She never got that close. "Babies cry." Her voice came out in a whisper, slightly harsh. She cleared her throat. "Toby probably cries less than most. He's a happy baby."

"I wasn't criticizing." Intense blue eyes stared

into her own. She struggled for breath. "I just didn't know. I wouldn't even know what was normal for a baby. No experience."

Somehow she managed to nod, her head feeling oddly wobbly on her body. She needed to back away, to quit staring into those mesmerizing eyes. She was making a fool of herself. That was so not acceptable.

Colleen took a step backward away from Dillon. It wasn't far enough. She still felt locked in that blue gaze.

One more step.

He lowered his gaze slightly, turned down the intensity. "So, he's happy?"

Ah, back in safe territory. She managed a small smile as she turned back and began moving toward the room again. "Come see. He's especially cheerful and cuddly when he first wakes up. As long as he wakes up on his own timetable, that is."

She stepped through the doorway and Dillon came up beside her. Toby was on his stomach, and as soon as he saw Colleen his crying turned to a soulful whimpering. His gaze slipped over to Dillon, and a look of distress came over his face.

Dillon sucked in a visible breath. Colleen felt for him. A man's first meeting with his child should be a wondrous thing, not a sad one.

"He's scared of me."

"He hasn't seen many men, and you're a rather

large one. You have a deeper voice. You might need to soften it and speak more quietly at first to keep from startling him."

Toby was visibly upset now.

"I've made him cry more. You should pick him up."

"Ordinarily I would," she agreed, "but right now we need to soothe him without upsetting him, and if I pick him up and then turn him over to you, he'll howl for sure."

"What should I do then? I don't want to hurt him or scare him more than he is."

Colleen didn't really know. She loved babies. She particularly loved *this* baby. Still, she ran on pure instinct most of the time the same way she did with her horses or other animals. She had always had terrible instincts where men were concerned; awful luck. She'd made very bad decisions or had others' bad choices thrust on her, but this was one decision she couldn't afford to muck up. Despite the fact that Dillon was going to take Toby away from her soon, she couldn't sacrifice the child in a lame attempt to make the man retreat.

"Stay close to me," she told Dillon. "Toby's used to me, and he's…well, he's very young. Maybe if he associates you with me, an extension of sorts, he'll accept you more quickly."

"Will that work?"

"Maybe."

She heard what sounded like a low curse and looked to her side.

"Sorry," he said. "I'll have to train myself not to do that. I've been living the life of a soldier too long."

Colleen nodded. She couldn't begin to imagine what his life had been like, what kind of hell he had been living in when his leg had been damaged so badly. And she didn't want to. She was doing all this for Toby, she told herself. Not for Dillon.

But as she moved toward the crib, she slowed enough so that Dillon could stay with her without lurching too much. Reaching the crib, she turned to Dillon. "I'm going to soothe him a bit. Just stay close, speak quietly and don't make any sudden movements."

Dillon didn't answer. His gaze was locked on his child.

She reached down and stroked her thumb across Toby's cheeks, smoothing away the tears that were rolling down his tiny face. "It's all right, sweetheart," she said. "This is your daddy. He just wants to meet you."

Quietly, quietly, she spoke, she caressed, she slowly felt Toby begin to relax. He stopped crying.

"All right, you touch him now," she told Dillon. "Gently."

And suddenly she was very aware of how close she and Dillon were standing. His warmth was up against her. She breathed in, and the scent of his aftershave filled her senses, pungent and male and…her hand trembled slightly.

Dillon reached out and placed his big hand next to hers. Toby was small, and Dillon's thumb brushed against her fingers.

Colleen felt suddenly dizzy. Every nerve ending in her body snapped to attention. She swallowed.

"I'm going to let go now," she whispered, turning to her left. She looked up and found her lips only a breath away from Dillon's.

Don't feel. Don't even dare to think of him as anyone who could ever be important to you, she ordered herself. Men had brought her nothing but pain. Her father who had taken risks and had died suddenly, breaking her heart. Her stepfather and stepbrother who had verbally abused and taunted her, making her life a misery. The man who had pretended to love her, but had really loved her land and had left her for a wealthier woman.

She'd been caught by surprise when each of those relationships had bitten her, but with Dillon, she already knew he was too great a risk. Allowing herself to feel anything, even simple lust, was just setting herself up for disaster. She couldn't face that kind of crippling disappointment again.

Slowly, Colleen forced herself to breathe, to enforce control over her reactions.

She tried a simple, shaky smile.

"I'm ready," Dillon said.

Colleen blinked, then realized that he was referring to flying solo with Toby.

She lifted her hand off the baby's warm back. When she glanced down, he was staring at her and Dillon with those big blue solemn eyes. Quietly considering the situation.

The baby shifted his attention to Dillon.

His lower lip quivered. He let out a cry.

"Oh, Toby," she said, then automatically turned to Dillon to explain that things would get better soon.

But Dillon wasn't paying attention. He automatically reached down and lifted the little bundle into his arms, curving Toby into his big body.

"I've got you, slugger," he said. "And I won't ever hurt you. I won't let you down or leave you. I won't let anyone harm you. Ever." His words were a low, quiet whisper. He stared into those blue eyes, cupping the baby close. "You're mine, Toby," he said. "We're father and son. We're going to be buddies and make our own little world, just you and me."

On and on he went, that deep, soothing baritone whispering promises, bits of nothing. It didn't matter, because the baby was reacting to the secure hold Dillon had on him and the hypnotic tone of his voice. Slowly, Toby stilled, quieted.

"Are we good, buddy?" Dillon asked.

As if he understood the question, Toby let out a watery coo.

Dillon looked over the baby's head straight into Colleen's eyes. His smile was brilliant, gorgeous and oh so sexy. "You're one heck of a teacher, Colleen," he said.

The smile went right through her, and her body reacted as if she were on a thrill ride. Out of control, her heart flipped right up into her throat, sending pleasure through her even though she knew there would eventually be a sudden drop that would bang her about. A man who could so easily produce a reaction like that must have been one heck of a commander, one heck of a CEO, one very talented…

The word *lover* came to mind, but she blanked it out of her mind. That smile of his, that darn smile…

I am in so much trouble, she thought. On so many levels.

CHAPTER THREE

DILLON stepped out on the porch and found Colleen trying to open up a sleeper sofa that looked as if it hadn't been used during the past century. The mechanical parts were putting up a good fight as Colleen tugged.

"I don't mean to insult you," Dillon said. "Given the fact that you run a ranch, you're clearly capable and probably strong, too, but…"

He reached down and touched Colleen's hand. Her skin was softer than he would have expected from a woman who did physical labor. Caught off guard, his body immediately reacted to that softness, that warmth, this woman. The fact that they were standing next to what was going to be his bed didn't help the situation any. Irritated with himself, Dillon put the brakes on his reaction to the best of his ability.

Colleen must have had her mind elsewhere, because as his words faded away and as he moved up beside her, she let out a tiny gasp and let go of the metal handle, backing up a step. Good. He didn't want to continue to be that aware of her. He definitely didn't need to be thinking erotic thoughts about her.

"I didn't mean to startle you," he said, as he gave a tug on the handle and the bed pulled partway out.

"You're not supposed to be doing that," she said.

He looked over his shoulder at her as he lowered the legs of the bed to the ground. "Why?" he asked, turning to face her.

She hesitated. He knew that she was thinking of his cane and his injury. He hated that.

"You're…you're a guest," she said.

"I'm an intruder."

"That would only be true if I hadn't agreed for you to stay, but I did. I'm totally in control of the situation."

He smiled at that.

"What?"

"I don't think either of us is in control of the situation. You had a baby dumped on you out of the blue. I had a wife who divorced me, then kept my child from me. Now you've, unexpectedly, been asked to house a man when it's obvious that that's not something you and your employees are used to."

A small smile lifted her lips.

"What?" he asked.

"That was so polite the way you put that, the fact that we're not used to having men around. As you could see from some of the women's reactions, it's not that we dislike men. At least not all men. We've just…all of us have had bad experiences, so we're taking a break. Some for the short term and some for forever. Julie's on the road to being engaged, so her break's over and she'll most likely be leaving soon. But for the most part, yes, this place has become a bit of a haven for women who need to drop out of the bride game."

"I've never heard it called that."

"Me either. I just made it up. But it's true that even in this century, most women grow up thinking they'll probably eventually get married."

"You?"

Her smile seemed to freeze. "I had a little more unconventional upbringing. I lost my father early, my stepfather and stepbrother were, to put it nicely, bullies without souls and my failed engagement…well, let's just say that I have major trust issues and I won't ever be a bride. I don't want to be. So, I guess you were right, after all. I do steer clear of men."

"Except for Toby."

"He's a baby."

"He won't always be a baby."

"I know." She sounded sad.

"You don't want him to grow up?"

"Of course I do. I just—I won't…he's yours, Dillon. Not mine."

She wouldn't see him grow up.

"I'm sorry about that." And he was. Genuinely.

She cared about Toby, and already Dillon was inclined to think favorably of anyone who liked his child.

"It's not your fault," she told him. "You'll take him away when you go, and if I were in your shoes…if he were mine, nothing would stop me from taking him home and claiming him. You shouldn't even think about apologizing for that, just as I'm not going to apologize about the fact that I'll miss him when he's gone."

"Good. I prefer honesty." He'd had too little of that with Lisa. Or maybe he'd been the one lying, thinking they were a match when they were no more suited than he and Colleen Applegate were.

She nodded. "Well then, the honest truth is that this bed is probably *not* almost comfortable as I implied earlier. Looking at it now, I'd say you're going to have a very restless night."

He shrugged. His comfort was the least of his worries these days. "I assume you'll want to lock the door, but will you call me if you need me in the night?"

For a second those dark eyes looked startled and sensually aware. That wouldn't do. Not when he was already too aware of her as a woman. His concentration from here on out had to be on Toby. Unlike his parents, he would put his child first. He would actually care. His choices would be made carefully, logically. No whisking women in and out of his life. No risking Toby getting attached to someone who was temporary. In fact, no more risking making the kind of mistakes he'd made with Lisa. Besides, Colleen definitely wasn't the kind of woman who would welcome a drive-by fling. Apparently she wouldn't welcome any kind of fling. A good thing.

"I won't need to call you. I've been handling things for three months," she argued.

"Yes. But I'm here now."

For several seconds they stood there, toe-to-toe. It was obvious that she didn't want to give up her control. Maybe it was because of those soulless men she'd known. No matter. He sympathized but he couldn't compromise with his son.

"I'll call you if there's an emergency," she said.

Which wasn't exactly the same thing, but it would do. He and Colleen were going to be tangling with each other for the entire time he was here, Dillon thought.

It should have made him angry. Instead he was intrigued.

Watch it, he told himself. *This woman is fire.*

Unfortunately, he seemed to be attracted to fire, because when she turned to leave he had an insane urge to call her back.

Dillon lay on the sleeper sofa the next morning and scrubbed one hand through his hair. He was tense and uneasy in more ways than one and none of them had much to do with the bumpy metal frame of the sleeper sofa biting into his back.

No, sleeping on Colleen's porch last night, he had discovered that the walls of the house were thin. There might be a door separating him from the building, but with the porch only covered by a screen, he'd been privy to a view of the windows. Even with the extremely faint and undefined shadow showing through on her light-dimming window shade, he'd been able to tell that Colleen's bedroom was just off to his left. He'd heard her humming and had been unable to think of anything except for the fact that she was getting ready for bed.

Heat had seared him as he'd tried to force himself to think about the business matters he needed to tend to when he had time tomorrow.

And when he'd awakened moments ago, his first instinct had been to look toward Colleen's window. His first thought had been to wonder if she realized how her silhouette had fueled his fantasies.

Don't be an idiot, he told himself. The woman had a ranch to run, a baby to take care of, employees to supervise and a clueless man to train as a father. She had too many things on her plate to add seduction to the list. Besides, there wasn't a coy bone in her body that he could tell, and with her ranch located off the beaten path, no one would, under ordinary circumstances, ever see anything at all. If she even thought about the possibility that he'd caught a glimpse of her body's outline on the shade, he knew she'd be appalled. She was already uneasy about him being in the house. Those pretty caramel eyes of hers might spark amber when she looked at him, but if not for Toby, she would never have let him into her house at all. This ranch was clearly a hideout for wounded women and Colleen's reasons for mistrusting men seemed to go deep.

He understood her need to steer clear of unwise entanglements. Caring for Toby, making sure he had free and clear custody of Toby and preserving his business for Toby was all Dillon could concern himself with from now on.

With that admission, he shoved himself up off the couch, slipped on his jeans, got up and knocked on the door.

When Colleen opened it, she was wearing a white fluffy bathrobe that had seen better days but still reminded him that she had only recently been lying in bed. Her hair was slightly tousled as if some man had plunged his fingers into all those untamed curls. With that image, Dillon's good intentions took a nosedive. Somehow he forced a good-morning smile to his lips.

She smiled back, even though he noticed that her hands were fidgeting with her belt.

"Where's Toby?" he asked, trying to get his mind back on track.

"He's a very early riser, so he's already been up for a while and had his breakfast."

Dillon frowned. "I should be doing that. Feeding him, I mean. I'll have to get up earlier. I apologize."

She wrinkled her nose. "Don't apologize. It's your first full day of daddyhood. Besides, I love being the one to give him his first meal of the day. He's so alert and fun to watch. Not that I won't willingly turn the task over to you. You have the right, and yes, you need to get used to his hours, but for today, it's fine. Millie's reading to him."

Dillon lifted a brow. "Isn't he a little young for books?"

She laughed, the sound deep and husky and delicious. "You say that as if he's already graduated to sneaking the underwear sections of the Sunday ads. Babies like to be cuddled, and while they're being cuddled, they especially like listening to you and feeling your voice as it rumbles up through your body. Add in the bright colors of a picture book and you've got a winning activity. Plus, Millie loves reading to him as much as I do. She has children but they're all grown and none of them want to have kids."

An odd, sad sensation slipped through Dillon. "I'm lucky that you and Millie were the ones to take him in. Not every woman would have cared for him the way the two of you have." Including, apparently, Toby's mother.

"I think most people, when faced with a child in need, grow to love that child at least a little."

"That hasn't been my experience."

She blinked, and he realized that he had let something slip that he had never shared, because he wasn't referring only to Lisa's treatment of Toby but his own childhood experiences. Bad move. It was the kind of remark that seemed to require an explanation, but he wasn't prepared to share more than he had already offered, so he merely shook his head, dismissing his hasty words.

Colleen looked troubled but she merely nodded. "You'll probably want to spend as much time as possible with Toby today. I think just being with him and letting him get used to you will be enough for one day. You're the first male in his life, so after you've had breakfast and taken a shower or whatever else you need to do, I'll let Millie know that you're on dad duty until nap time. She'll step in if he needs his diaper changed. Later today will be soon enough to tackle the big stuff."

"You think I can't handle it yet?"

Her lips curved up in an entrancing smile. "You told me you'd slept in the mud, so I'm sure you can handle a little mess. I'm just not sure if Toby's ready to be traumatized by a crooked diaper yet."

Dillon couldn't help smiling back at her. "Already criticizing my skills, Colleen?"

"Everyone needs practice. Have fun." With that, she turned toward the back of the house. When she came back a few minutes later, Dillon was finishing his breakfast. He looked up.

Colleen was wearing blue jeans that weren't exceptionally tight, but that emphasized the length of her legs and the curve of her hips. The cherry-red shirt tucked into the jeans fit where a shirt should fit a woman. She was wearing some sort of green polished glass on a black satin cord around her neck, and he remembered seeing it yesterday, too. In fact, there seemed to be a lot of brightly colored polished glass in the house. Sun catchers and wind chimes hung here and there, the golds and reds and blues and greens turned warm by the light.

"I have to go into town for supplies," she said, "but I'll stop in before I head out onto the range again. Toby will go down in an hour or so. Then he'll take another nap this afternoon, so if you have other things to do, that would be a good time to see to them."

"Don't worry about me. I'll figure it out or I'll ask Millie. Toby and I will be great. Everything's fine." Except for the fact that he had—again—noticed too many things about Colleen that he found attractive. What was wrong with him? He had no intention of getting into a long-term relationship with a woman again, so he needed to get this "problem" under control.

His phone rang, and Colleen gave him a wave as she headed for the door. Dillon looked down and wanted to swear. The call was from Lisa. She hadn't called him since she'd asked for a divorce and even then she hadn't called. He'd gotten the message in an e-mail. So why was she calling now?

Anger filled him. Lisa was one of those people who changed their minds about what to wear ten times and then spent all night worrying that they had made the wrong choice. Had she heard that he was coming to Montana to get Toby? How would she react to that? Would she change her mind and decide that *she* wanted the baby now?

By the time he'd decided that there was no point in speculating about anything at all about his ex-wife and never had been, the phone stopped ringing.

Ten seconds later, the phone in Colleen's house began to ring. She had already stepped onto the porch and was just closing the door, but she turned around, came back inside and looked at Dillon. Then she walked toward the phone and glanced at the number registered there.

Slowly, she raised her chin and looked into Dillon's eyes. "It's her," she said. She didn't have to say more.

"I realize that this is your house, but I just think you should know right now," he said, "that I'm not letting her near Toby."

Colleen frowned, those pretty brows drawing together. "You shouldn't drag your child into a battle between you and your ex-wife." Somehow, the way she said that made him think she had some experience of such things.

Slowly, Dillon shook his head. He walked over to her and stared down into her troubled eyes, taking her hands in his own. "This isn't about Lisa ending our marriage. We were people whose goals and interests were too different for us to stay married, and I should have realized that before I proposed. We weren't a logical fit, but I asked her to marry me, anyway, so I'll take my share of the blame for the failure of the marriage.

"But there's something else I can't forgive. She walked away from Toby when he had barely entered the world. She left him and didn't seem to care what became of him. It couldn't have been money. I gave her money in the settlement. She just didn't want him. She didn't even mention that he was on the way, so I'm not letting her change her mind and try to take him from me now. Especially not when she could change her mind again and do a one-eighty a few days later. What's more, I'm not apologizing even though I know she's someone from your past, so don't ask me to."

"You're forgetting that since I've known her longer, I may know even more of how she operates," Colleen said. "Lisa used to go through men like sticks of gum that lost their flavor quickly. The only time she came back to a guy the second time was when she thought he had something to offer her that she had overlooked the first time around." She kept her chin high as she stared directly into his eyes and dropped this nugget into the conversation.

"Yes, that was her on my cell phone," he told her, answering the question she hadn't asked. "So, I'm one of those men she's contacted a second time. What do you think she's overlooked that she's come back for? Do you think she's developed an urge to raise a baby?"

Colleen's smile grew taut. "I'll help you," she said.

"Why?"

She hesitated, then let out a deep, audible breath. "I suppose I have lots of reasons and some of them aren't exactly admirable, but the main one is that Toby is a sweet, adorable little boy and…Dillon, he's just a baby. A total innocent. No one should get to dump him and then turn around and pretend it never happened. When she left here, she didn't even leave any way for me to get in touch with her in case something happened to him. It was…I don't know…as if she didn't even care."

He digested that bit of information, and indignation for the child in the other room seared his soul. Toby wasn't old enough to know his mother had abandoned him at birth but someday he *would* be old enough to realize the truth, and that would hurt him. Dillon wanted to swear, but he was a guest here and he needed to behave.

"Are you going to call her back?" Colleen asked.

"No. Sooner or later I'll have to talk to her, but not today. I have other calls to make while Toby's sleeping. Things to do with my firm."

Colleen looked slightly uncomfortable. She fidgeted with her belt buckle. "I'm sure you have lots of things to do, business you need to get back to, and during the night, it occurred to me…"

He waited.

"Babies sleep a lot. There's a lot of down-time," she said. "And you're a man who's used to being busy."

Dillon raised a brow. "How did you reach that conclusion?"

"You were a soldier who led other soldiers. You built structures and started running a company when you were barely out of college and still going to grad school. That's all in your bio on the Farraday Engineering Web site. In fact, I think one of the articles said something about how you specialized in multitasking, but ranch life moves at a slower pace. That could be a problem. You might get bored here really fast."

"Meaning I might want to leave here after only a few days."

"Yes."

"And take my son with me."

Her eyes looked stricken. "Yes."

"Maybe we should set a specific date. I do need to make sure that I know what I'm doing as a father, and I'm more than grateful that you've agreed to help me with that, but I can't stay here too long. Being an absentee owner of a business has drawbacks, and while I did my best to take charge when I was bedridden, now that I'm mobile, it's past time for me to take back the helm of the firm. If I name a time frame, at least you'll know when the end is coming. Will that be best?"

Slowly she nodded.

"Three weeks?" he asked.

"That sounds good." But her voice was a bit tight. Obviously, letting go of Toby would be difficult for her. "Now," she continued, "is there anything you need while I'm in town? Something that will make the hours when Toby's napping pass more quickly? Books? Newspapers?"

He laughed. "Pamper the rich, bored male, you mean? Eventually there will be things I'll need, but I'm not sure what will be on the list and when I know, I'll have everything delivered."

She looked startled. "That won't be necessary. I have a pickup truck."

"Yes, but I don't think a load of lumber and roofing shingles will fit in your truck."

"Lumber and shingles? I don't understand."

Dillon smiled. "I'm more than just a rich man, Colleen. I'm an engineer. I know how to build things and build them right. I can fix your porch."

She blushed prettily. "I'm afraid I can't afford it right now."

"I can."

"But you're a—"

He put his finger over her lips to stop her from saying *guest*.

"You're helping me. Let me help *you*. I'm going to do this," he said. "And a few other things, starting with replacing that sleeper sofa."

Now, he had her attention. She crossed her arms over chest, which was supposed to make her look stern, he was sure, but only served to draw his attention to her pretty breasts. "I can't let you do that much," she said.

"You can't stop me, Colleen. I'm a man on a mission. Now go do whatever you need to do."

And stop looking so adorable, he thought as she walked away.

CHAPTER FOUR

How am I going to survive this man? Colleen thought as she drove toward town. He had only been here less than a day and already he seemed to fill up her house.

What's more, when she got to town she found that word of Dillon's arrival had already spread. "Buying a lot of food, are you? Stocking up?" Alma Anderson asked at the grocery store. "Yeah, a man will eat you out of house and home, especially if he's a big man. *Is* he a big man? Is he staying long?"

Colleen pasted on a smile that didn't say anything but seemed to satisfy Alma.

"Wow, I can't remember the last time I associated the word *man* with you, Colleen," Barb Seltzer added. She was getting ready to expound on that and probably ask more questions when Colleen cut in.

"Sorry, gotta run, ladies. Business to tend to."

But it was the same everywhere she went. The

town had never had anyone rich in their midst, at least not anyone who was planning to stay more than a day or two. "I saw that car when he drove through town yesterday," Bill Winters said with a long, low whistle. "A man would do a lot for a sleek, fast car like that. A brand-new Ferrari? Pricey. I never thought to see one in Bright Creek. So…that guy at the house, this Dillon Farraday, Lisa's man, I guess he's pretty used to having the best, eh?"

"Um," Colleen muttered, loading the rest of her supplies into the truck.

"Of course he's used to the best," Harve Enson said. "He married Lisa, didn't he? And Lisa was the best we had to offer. Certainly the prettiest I always thought. Lisa was the Lupine Festival queen, wasn't she? And the homecoming queen? She was the lead in all those plays and had the most boyfriends before she ran off to Chicago to go to college. You went out with her, didn't you, Rob?" he asked his son, who had just come out of the hardware store next door.

"Who?" Rob asked.

"Lisa Breckinridge."

"I went out with her once, before she started dating that college guy three years older. Why do you want to know?"

"Her ex-husband is staying with Colleen."

Rob raised his eyebrows and looked at Colleen

as if Harve had just announced that she was really from an alien planet. "I don't get it. Why is he doing that?"

"He's come for his baby, Rob, not for me," she said between gritted teeth. It was patently obvious that Rob couldn't think of any reason a good-looking man would be visiting her.

"I didn't mean that in a bad way," Rob mumbled, and to his credit, he blushed and looked uncomfortable. "I just…I mean…"

"Forget it, Rob," she said, letting him off the hook.

"The point is," Harve continued, "the man is used to champagne." Harve suddenly looked at what Colleen was doing.

"Colleen, I don't know why you're buying so much stuff. He's come for his kid and how long will that take? A man like that won't want to stay in a little do-nothing town like Bright Creek. For sure he won't want to stick around long on a little horse ranch. No disrespect, Colleen," he said. "You're the best horsewoman around and you rent out the best fishing pond of anyone, but unless this guy's a fisherman, there's not much of what he's used to at your place."

Which seemed to be the general consensus and was, in fact, the truth, so Colleen shouldn't let it sting so much.

"We'll see," Colleen said. "He's staying for three weeks, so I'd appreciate it if you'd all stop gossiping about him. If we don't act like do-nothings and gossips, he won't think that's what we are." Hastily, she threw the rest of her things in the truck and headed for the driver's side door.

"Three weeks? What's he going to do?"

She kept moving. She was *so* not going to bring Toby further into this than she already had. Dillon probably didn't want to broadcast the news that he had asked her to give him lessons in something most people considered basic knowledge. Announcing that might embarrass him, which might result in him leaving and taking Toby away from her immediately.

Besides, while everyone already knew that Toby was Lisa's son and that she had been married to Dillon, they also knew Dillon had been away at war last year. And so far no one had openly questioned the paternity of Lisa's child. *At least not in my presence,* Colleen thought. Maybe because Lisa apparently still held legend status here despite leaving her baby with Colleen. Maybe they assumed—or hoped—Lisa had a good reason for deserting him. So, if it protected Dillon and Toby, Colleen could live with the lie that Lisa was the best of Bright Creek. That meant not even venturing near the topic of Toby, Dillon and Lisa any more than she had to.

"He says he's going to fix things on the ranch."

Harve and Bill exchanged looks. "By himself?

Colleen, hon, did you explain to him how long that place has been falling down around your ears?"

No, she had not. She still had some pride, and the beginning of the demise of the ranch house went back to the worst time of her life, when her mother had remarried and brought darkness to their lives. It was not something she wanted to drop into a conversation with Dillon.

"Dillon says he can do it," she said. But as she started to open the door, she heard words that she wished she hadn't.

"A one-man reclamation team raising those old buildings from the dead? This I have to see. Besides, if he's going to be here for a while, I sure would like to take a ride in that car."

Harve told Rob what Dillon had been driving, and Rob let out a low whistle. "Man, that's sweet."

"Yeah, I wonder if he'll let us inside it."

"I don't think—" she began. But Harve and Bill were already walking away, lost in their plans. And even Rob, who was still standing on the sidewalk, had a speculative gleam in his eyes.

Uh-oh, Colleen thought as she got in the truck and drove away. If one person came, more would follow. Colleen had a feeling that Dillon hadn't counted on having an audience gawking while she instructed him. And as the woman who had uttered the words that were surely the start to the Bright Creek equivalent of the Gold Rush, it was up to her to head off the townspeople and divert their attention from Dillon. The man needed to learn to change diapers, not give test drives of his car.

He's not going to thank me for this, she thought.

The sight that met Colleen's eyes when she drove up to the house made her heart flip around and her breath catch in her throat. Dillon stood next to her porch, which was already looking sturdier. He was shirtless, a hammer was snagged in the back belt loop of his jeans and he was holding Toby up against his naked chest. He was, in short, gorgeous. A man feast for a woman's eyes, the best the male species had to offer visually. A lot of bests in Dillon's world, Colleen thought. His car. His ex-wife.

Darn it! For half a second, Harve's words about Lisa being the best slipped in before Colleen hastily tromped that sucker of a thought down. As a woman who had been hurt too much and who wasn't most men's idea of perfect femininity, she might not want to enter into the bride game, but she still liked to look, and no way was she going to let thoughts of Lisa spoil this brief, perfect moment.

Dillon looked up and smiled, those ice-blue eyes focused on her. "Welcome back," he said.

She couldn't help smiling at him even though she knew it wasn't smart to make these exchanges a habit. They left her too warm and yearning for things she could never have.

"This isn't finished," he said, indicating the porch that certainly already looked much straighter than it had. "Might take a few days. Until then, you'll need to use the side door."

Colleen nodded slowly. She wasn't sure where to look. His direct blue gaze was compelling. His bare chest made her feel even warmer than she should on such a warm day. The fact that she wanted to step closer made her feel as if she really should take a step back. In the end, her dilemma was solved when Toby began to babble and buck and hold out his arms to her.

"Little traitor," Dillon said affectionately, winking at his son, and just like that he lifted Toby, dropped a kiss on the top of his silky baby hair and turned him so that the baby could see Colleen better. "Don't worry, big guy. She'll have some time for you, I'm sure. See there, I told you she'd be back."

Toby's response was to blow a bubble and wave his arms around.

But entranced as she was with the child she loved, it was the man's easy manner with him that held her attention. Dillon had never had a child. Most men would be at least a little tentative at first. The new fathers she'd met always were. But not Dillon. Toby looked totally right and comfortable held against his daddy's big body.

Big, half-naked body, Colleen thought, then immediately wished she could keep a lid on her thoughts.

"I need to put a shirt on now that I'm done for the day," he said as if he'd read her mind. He looked down at Toby, then at Colleen, a question in his eyes. "Not that I'm abdicating my paternal responsibilities or anything, mind you, or that I'm foisting him off on you, but..."

"Here," she said with a smile and reached out to take Toby from him. "As if I'd complain. He's a treasure. Right?" she asked the baby, who promptly crowed and smiled and stuffed his fist in his mouth.

"Nothing like a compliment from a lady, is there, Toby?" Dillon asked as he snagged his shirt from the railing and slipped it over his shoulders. "Did you get everything you needed?"

"Yes, but I need to talk to you about something."

"Not a problem. Why don't you show me a bit of the ranch? I'll get a hat for the big guy here."

"I'm impressed. Most men wouldn't have thought of the fact that a baby is more sensitive to the sun."

"Yes, well, don't give me too much credit. Millie's the one who reminded me. I could only bring him outside to sit with me if I promised to stay in the shade."

"But you learned quickly."

He laughed. "You should teach school. You're

good at giving pats on the back for small accomplishments."

"School? You must have been talking to someone. It's no secret around here that I've wanted to start a ranch camp for girls for several years. I'd especially like to be able to give at-risk girls from the city who've never been near a ranch the chance to see how empowering this life can be."

"Why don't you do it?"

She shrugged. "Money. A proper building for them to sleep in. Maybe a fear that I might not be good at it."

"Never know until you try, will you? Of course, that's easy for me to say, but it looks as if you've already made a start with Gretchen and Julie. Millie told me that their father was an abuser and you were aware of that when they came to work for you."

"Yes, but they *do* work here. And they'd grown up on a ranch. I didn't have to teach them anything or expose them to a lifestyle they'd never lived. All I did was give them a job."

"Is that all?" he asked, a teasing tone in his voice. "Just a job where they don't have to live in fear. Millie told me that you also gave *her* a place to stay when her husband died and left her with tons of debt."

"Millie makes more of things than actually

exist. Besides, the women are my friends. They give as much as they get, so even if their situation helped spawn the idea for the ranch camp, it's nothing like bringing girls here who've never even seen a horse and trying to teach them some basic skills. It's not the same as being in a situation where I might actually harm someone if I do or say the wrong thing. With Julie and Gretchen, there was nothing I needed to teach them about raising, riding or caring for horses."

"Just horses? I thought you were a cattle ranch."

"No. When my mother, stepfather and step-brother died in a small plane crash while I was at a rodeo, and the ranch passed to me, I sold the cattle and some of the land to pay bills. We're a small horse ranch with a number of sidelines. We have an orchard, we open our section of the creek to fly fisherman, Gretchen and Julie make and sell flies and Millie has a small bread-making business. Basically, if we have the time and know-how and we can make money off of it, we try it."

While they were talking, they made their way to a pasture where horses were grazing. One of them, a white one, whinnied and slowly ambled over to the fence.

"Hey, Mr. Peepers." Colleen shifted the baby to her side to keep him away from the horse and stroked the aging animal. "He's a sweetheart. Mr. Peepers and I did some fine barrel racing together."

"So, you're a cowgirl. A rodeo queen."

"I *am* a cowgirl, a horsewoman. These are my babies." Instantly, she wished she could call back the last comment. Already Dillon suspected the truth: that she couldn't have children and that it broke her heart. She'd seen it in his eyes when they'd discussed her desire for babies yesterday. And she didn't want him feeling sorry for her. There were enough people in town who already did that and always had. It set her apart and made her too different. It created barriers she'd never understood how to breach. She needed to turn the conversation in a different direction, so she might as well discuss what she'd brought him out here to say. "I love my life, Dillon, and my world here. I've made it all myself, and I'm responsible for whatever happens here. So, I have to tell you, I might have done something wrong and made a mistake when I went into town. One that will affect you."

She explained about Bill and Harve and Rob and the car. "I should have made them understand. Argued more. Made it clear that you weren't here to give tours of your Ferrari."

"Don't worry about it."

"No. I was the one who made the mistake. I want you to know that I won't let them come on my land to pester you."

"They're your neighbors."

"Doesn't matter. They're just being nosy. That's not right."

He turned her around and placed his hands on her shoulders, the baby between them. Her entire body felt as if it might melt at his touch. "When I leave here, you have to live with your friends and neighbors. It's only a car. I don't mind giving a test drive to a couple of your neighbors. Seriously not an issue with me."

She was still unconvinced. "They might ask a lot of gossipy questions about Toby and Lisa."

"Then I just won't answer. Do you always feel this responsible about everything that happens here?" he asked.

"No. Yes. I guess I feel I have to. This ranch is my whole world. It's what makes me who I am, and these people...the women...if *I* fail, they lose their livelihoods when they've all already had to face too many bad things in their lives."

"But it's me you're trying to protect this time."

She shrugged. "Maybe you could use a sanctuary for a few weeks, too. Just because you're rich doesn't mean you've been exempted from the tough stuff. It couldn't have been easy marrying Lisa and losing her. Or going to war. Or being wounded."

Toby had fallen asleep and was listing to one side in her arms. Without a word and with seemingly little effort, Dillon took him and tucked him against his shoulder. Then he reached out and slid one palm along Colleen's jaw.

He had a magic touch. She wanted to lean right into his palm, step up against his body. Instead, she forced herself to simply look into his eyes.

"I doubt that divorce is ever easy for anyone, but I've had a long time to think about it, and I think my marriage was doomed from the start. I can't even really blame Lisa. She has that princess aura, and I chose her thinking she would be a good wife for a businessman the way other men choose a suit off the rack. But she wanted someone more exciting than I was, someone more willing to make the rounds of the social circuit and less of a workaholic and I should have realized that from the start. When I got called back into service and went overseas, she was livid about the fact that I didn't fight my tour of duty. As for the rest…no, none of that was easy, but still easier than a lot of other people who went to war have had. From that perspective, I can't complain."

"Are you just being nice, trying to make me feel better and forget that I messed up? Because I *did* mention the car and your work on the ranch. Now Harve Enson thinks you're some foolish guy who's easy prey and he's going to stalk you just because he's bored and has nothing to do with his time."

He stared down into her eyes, his own that unsettling blue. "If I really wanted you to forget something, I'd try a more drastic approach."

"What?"

He shifted the baby and leaned into her, sweeping his arm around her waist. "I'm not easy prey," he whispered when his lips were just a breath away from hers. "What I am is curious. Maybe even a bit fascinated."

He touched his mouth to hers and his touch was so…hot, so…she didn't know what. It was like nothing she had ever felt before. Like jumping your horse over a barrier so high that you weren't sure you could land safely. Fear and elation and excitement all mixed together. And when it was over, there was definitely an insane desire to do that dangerous thing all over again, she thought as he pulled away, leaving her lips aching.

"That was…what was that about?" she asked.

"It was probably about following through on a bad idea even though you have an incredibly delicious mouth, Colleen."

Her lips were still burning. Her body was still aching. Now she knew what kissing him was like and what she'd been missing and would never have. Darn it, she'd have been better off not knowing that.

"We shouldn't do that again," she whispered.

"You're probably right. I seem to have bad luck with the women of Bright Creek. Probably best to keep my distance."

And just like that, she remembered one more reason why she had to stay smart about Dillon. He was temporary. He would leave her in the dust. He had never been for her and never would be. And thinking of him was only going to take her mind off her own concerns and very real goals of keeping the ranch running and saving money for the ranch camp.

"Let's go get the baby out of the sun and then later today, after I'm done with my work, I'll give you some more lessons," she said. "Some basic stuff."

"Basic. All right. I can handle that."

Hours later, Colleen was struggling to keep a straight face as Dillon stared down at his son and then looked at the diaper he held in his hand.

"An interesting contraption," he told his son.

Toby stared at him with those huge blue eyes and jabbered something unintelligible.

"The tabs go in the back and fasten in the front," Colleen said helpfully.

"Of course they do. Toby just told me so. Didn't you, buddy?"

Toby just stared.

"Oh sure, go quiet on me *now*," Dillon said. "Just when I'm looking for a little support here." He smiled, and Toby responded to his daddy's smile, giving a delighted little squeal.

"All right, then. Let's get this on you." Dillon lifted Toby's tiny bottom and slid the diaper under him. He brought the front of the diaper up and looked at the left of the diaper and then the right. He brought the sides of his hand up and sighted along it.

"The tabs…" Colleen began.

"I know. In the back, fasten in the front," Dillon repeated.

"Then what are you doing?" she asked gently.

"I'm measuring."

Colleen couldn't keep from chuckling. "Dillon, it's a diaper, not an engineering project."

Dillon gave her a patient, measured look. "Toby, she doesn't understand that we are men, and we have our own way of doing things."

"What she understands is that if you don't fasten that diaper on soon, Toby is going to respond to all this fresh air, and we'll have a lot of cleaning up to do," she said, raising a brow.

Dillon gave her a wry grin. "Have I mentioned what a wise woman Colleen is, scout?" he asked his son. "Of course, you already knew that. Let's get you diapered up."

When he was done, the diaper was almost perfectly straight, but not quite. He eyed it with a frown.

"Don't be so hard on yourself," she said. "You did great, and it's going to get easier…until he learns to crawl and wriggle away," she teased.

Dillon laughed. He scooped his son up into his

arms. "I can hardly wait." Then, his expression grew serious. "Thank you for helping me, Colleen. You're a good teacher."

"I didn't do anything."

"Yes. You did. He's happy. That's all you."

She wanted to tell him no, that Toby had been born a happy child, but her throat was closing up. She *needed* to ask him not to praise her, for fear she might do something foolish and take it too much to heart. She could not start yearning for praise from Dillon.

Finally, she found her voice. "Thank you," she said quietly. "I guess…it's time for Toby's story and bed. Then…I have some written material you might find helpful." Which was such a stupid, inane thing to say, but he nodded, took Toby and headed for the rocking chair.

Soon the sound of his deep, hypnotic voice could be heard in the kitchen where she had retreated so that Dillon could have some private time with his son.

She was alone in a way she hadn't been for the past three months. Maybe she'd never been this alone, Colleen thought. Because now she had experienced joy, a special kind of joy. And she craved it.

Get over it, she told herself. *Be happy with what you've been lucky enough to have been given. And stop moping. There's still a lot to do today. And maybe this would be a good day for you to go back to eating at the bunkhouse.* She was spending too much time alone with Dillon.

But by the time the day was done and the lessons were over, Millie had gone to bed with a headache, the women in the bunkhouse had made their own dinner and she and Dillon were all that was left.

"I'm not much of a cook, but I can manage something," she told him when he came back from putting Toby in his crib.

"I'd offer to do the honors, but I've never learned how."

"You've always had servants, haven't you?"

"It goes with the territory. My parents were too self-involved to cook. I was too busy. Fortunately, there are people who will cook for you if you pay them well."

She was pretty sure that he paid better than well. Before he'd come here she'd done her homework on him. She'd seen his name on one of those Web sites where people gossiped about which celebrities were lousy tippers at restaurants, and Dillon was a legendary highly generous tipper.

"I can help," he offered, but the thought of him being next to her while she cooked…after that kiss…well, she'd probably have a brain meltdown and slice off a finger or two.

"Go. Ramble. Read. Do something," she ordered.

He smiled and wandered out of the room. In a minute, she heard the noise of glass doors opening and closing and went to see what the commotion was. He had opened the china cabinet and was setting the table.

"You really are a rodeo queen." He motioned to the trophies and ribbons he'd had to move to get at the dishes.

"Well, everyone has to be good at one thing," she said.

He frowned at that. "I'm sure you're good at many things."

Automatically the sound of her stepfather telling her that she was good for absolutely nothing, that she was ugly and useless and that he couldn't believe someone as pretty as her mother had given birth to her, dropped in. She hadn't allowed that thought for ages.

"I was a great barrel racer back when I had the time to practice," she said as if she was trying to force that opinion down someone's throat.

"I would have liked to have seen that."

"I—" Colleen's words were cut off by the sound of Dillon's cell phone ringing.

He looked at the display. "Unfamiliar. Probably a wrong number, but…"

He clicked it on. Colleen went back into the kitchen to give him privacy.

"What's this about, Lisa? Yes, I know you called

earlier. You're in Europe. Fine. Where am I? I'm with my son."

Lisa, Colleen thought. Maybe Lisa wanted the baby even though she hadn't asked one question about him these past few months. Or maybe she wanted Dillon again. A woman like Lisa tended to get the things she wanted.

With an extra dollop of force, Colleen slammed the pan onto the stove.

"Lisa, we haven't talked in a year. What exactly do you want now?" Dillon continued. "I see. Well, you do what you have to do."

Colleen took out another pan and banged it on the stove, too. She wanted to scream, "Tell her not to call you here." But she didn't.

"I'd say this conversation is over," Dillon said.

Another pan. And another. And…

Colleen sensed rather than saw Dillon come into the room. She whirled and looked at him. He was leaning casually against the far wall, as if he'd been there all day and could stand there for another entire day. He looked as if nothing at all had happened.

"How can you be so calm?" she asked.

"I'm not, but tonight I'm too tired to think and react logically, and at the moment I have no recourse other than to keep tabs on her whereabouts. I already knew she was in Europe before she told me."

"What did she want?"

"She seemed to want to tell me that she'd been planning to come back to the States, but that she didn't have enough cash to make the trip and I—"

He paused.

"What?"

"How are we going to eat all this?"

Colleen looked down and saw that she had taken at least six pans out of the cabinet. They were squeezed together on the big commercial stove.

"I was angry," she said. "Really angry." She suddenly couldn't help smiling. "If Lisa had been here, I would have..."

"You would have what? Fed her to death?"

Colleen's smile grew. "Hey, I said that I wasn't a good cook, but nobody ever died from my cooking."

"I'm oddly reassured."

But Colleen wasn't. Standing here alone in the kitchen with Dillon, she felt vulnerable. He'd asked her earlier today what she was good at, but at this moment, staring at him across the room this way, all she could concentrate on were his lips. She wanted to be good at kissing Dillon Farraday. She wanted to forget that any adults other than the two of them even existed and she wanted him to kiss her again.

And since that wasn't going to happen, Colleen simply opened the refrigerator, pulled out a little of this and a little of that and hastily made two sandwiches. She handed one to Dillon.

"I do happen to make a darn good sandwich," she told him, trying to turn her thoughts back to the mundane.

"Looks delicious. I'll be sure to savor it." Which certainly didn't sound as mundane as it should have. In fact, when she woke in the middle of the night from a sound sleep, she realized that she had been dreaming that she and Dillon had been locked in a fierce embrace.

Surely it was just the newness of having a man in the house. "Tomorrow I will be so over this phase," she promised herself. No more thinking about Dillon beyond teaching him his duties.

CHAPTER FIVE

DILLON awoke to the sound of hushed whispers in the other part of the house. That was Colleen's low husky voice. Already he knew it. Already he was regretting having touched her...and yet not regretting it at all. For all her tough cowgirl ways, there was something very soft and vulnerable about her. And her skin was equally soft, her lips warm and womanly.

And my mind is where it has no business being, he thought. There were too many things to do today, too many important things to tend to. And some things he needed to talk to Colleen about. Despite his seemingly calm demeanor last night, Lisa's sudden reappearance worried him. Lisa, he'd discovered early in their marriage, had a reason for everything she did. She was good at masking her ambition behind a smiling facade but she was very ambitious. All his instincts told him she wanted money, and the tool she might use as leverage was a baby.

All that had passed through his mind last night, but he'd put off telling Colleen because…maybe because he hadn't wanted to upset her.

That wasn't like him. He had never shied from getting right to the tough stuff. When he'd been growing up, the only way to get his parents' attention had been to aim right for the jugular and cut directly to the heart of whatever topic he'd needed to take care of. He'd been that way ever since and it had stood him well in business and in war. Even in his personal life, he had jumped right in, met and married Lisa within a matter of weeks. But with Colleen, who had erected barriers the minute she'd met him and didn't have any qualms about making him abide by rules, he thought, looking at the offending door that separated him from her, he found himself wanting to ease into topics. With her shields up, she was hard to read at times, so going slowly was important. She tried to be tough. He knew she was strong in many ways, but he also sensed that she could be easily wounded. He could fail her, and he didn't want to either hurt her or fail her, not when he was pretty darn sure that she'd had more than her share of men doing that kind of thing.

But we still have to talk about things, he thought. Money and attention were Lisa's weaknesses, he'd learned. And now that he was back on his feet and able to be approached about giving her more funding, Lisa was probably going to be trouble. He would need to protect Toby. Things could get ugly, and he didn't want any of this spilling over onto Colleen. Unfortunately, given her affection for Toby, he wasn't sure how to protect her. Anger that the woman he had once trusted enough to marry might betray him again and roll over Colleen in the process made him want to swear.

Blowing out a breath, he rolled over, grabbed his clothes and got dressed. Then he padded to the door and gave a rap.

The door opened and he found himself facing Millie holding Toby, who had milk on his face, partially running down his bare baby chest and trickling into his diaper. The baby perked up and made happy smacking noises when he saw Dillon.

Dillon's heart flipped right over, and he held out his arms. Millie handed over Toby.

"Looks like breakfast was a winner," Dillon said, giving his child a kiss. "It also looks like I'll be taking my first lesson on giving you a bath."

Millie chuckled, but he wondered why she was the one feeding Toby. Colleen had told him only yesterday how much she liked feeding Toby his breakfast.

"Where's Colleen?" he asked.

Millie hesitated.

"Is this one of those 'none of my business, because it has nothing to do with me' occasions?" he asked.

No. The answer was clearly no, even though Millie didn't speak. Her hesitation told him that Colleen's absence *did* have something to do with him. Did this have something to do with that thing about the car Colleen had mentioned yesterday? And if he asked, would he get an answer?

Fire fast and catch her off guard, he thought. *She'll either tell you something or think you're totally crazy.*

He smiled down at his son, then quickly turned toward Millie. "Is there any chance there are visitors coming today?" he asked with as much of a frown as he could muster with a baby pulling on the button of his shirt and slobbering on his arm as Toby bent over and tried to chew without teeth. "Colleen seemed to think my car might bring some…um…crazed fans out of the woodwork."

Millie's eyes opened wide. "Now, you're not to worry. As soon as the first man showed up a few minutes ago, Colleen headed down to the entrance to make sure no one tried to sneak up here."

"She's guarding the Ferrari?"

"I wouldn't exactly say guarding. Just telling everyone to back off. People are curious, but Colleen says that you and Toby are our guests, you're our responsibility and she doesn't want those men bothering you when you and Toby need some quality bonding time. Jokes might be made. Or they might try to coerce you to let them drive your car. In other words, she feels that our neighbors aren't minding their manners. But don't worry. She has her shotgun, and Colleen hardly ever misses."

Dillon blinked.

"Dillon, I'm just kidding, hon," Millie drawled. "Not about Colleen hardly ever missing, but about her having her gun. Colleen doesn't *need* a gun, but she *is* down there reading the riot act to the locals who came out to poke around and ask you nosy questions."

Which was totally wrong. She had done him a favor loving and caring for his child for the past three months, and now she was teaching him how to be a good father despite the fact that he was taking Toby away from her. Last night she had patiently sat down with him and given him a crash course on car seats and other safety issues. She had shepherded him through his first diaper change and assured him that Toby would let him know if he got the thing on too tight.

Dillon looked down at his son's milky face and gave him a kiss. "I'll be back," he said and he held Toby out to Millie. "Can you man the baby while I go give Colleen a hand?"

"You can't do that. You're supposed to be a—"

"Don't say *guest*. Everyone keeps saying that. That's an order."

Millie shrugged. "Sorry. We're just trying to be hospitable."

"And I appreciate it. But things will run more smoothly if you simply accept the fact that I'm used to taking charge and being responsible for my own actions and welfare. I'm not good at being a taker. At least I hope not. Now, where will I find her?"

"Probably down where the entrance to the Applegate is. Colleen won't stop the fishermen from going through, but she'll want to make sure that no one decides to wander up to the house to snoop around."

He nodded. "Toby?"

"Of course," Millie said. "And…thank you. It's nice that there's some man who doesn't automatically assume that Colleen should be capable of doing everything. People have always taken advantage of the fact that she's a doer. She takes on too much. Not that I should complain. If she hadn't been the kind of person she is and taken us in, who knows what would have happened to us, but…yeah, I'm glad you're not simply taking her for granted the way everyone in town seems to."

Interesting. Dillon was certainly going to find out more about that topic when he got a few minutes, but for now, it seemed that Colleen was off fighting dragons for him. He was grateful, but he just wasn't a dependent sort of guy. Couldn't ever be.

As he started out the door, Millie called to him. "The fastest way to the entrance is straight across the south pasture and through the orchard. If you take the road, it's a lot farther."

"Thank you," he said as he took off toward the entrance. Despite the uneven ground and his uncooperative leg, he moved as swiftly as he could, given that he had left his cane behind. He wasn't sure what this was all about, but he knew this much. If he weren't here, Colleen wouldn't have to take care of the extra work of making sure he wasn't "bothered." Which was crazy, given the fact that he *was* bothered and hot and all kinds of attracted to her every time she got close to him. A man wanting to ask him about his car? Or even watching him struggle with a diaper? That was easy stuff. Not wanting to touch Colleen? Far too difficult.

When he entered the orchard, the first thing he noticed was a striking sculpture of metal and what looked like broken bits of glass. It glittered in the sun, the glass tinkling in the breeze. Other bits of colored glass hung from the trees amidst the glossy leaves, the budding fruit and the gnarled branches. It was a bit like a living art gallery, but Dillon didn't stop, because midway through the orchard he heard Colleen's voice.

"Harve, now I know you didn't come here to fish. You only fish on Saturdays and the occasional Sunday. If you're here during the week, it's to spy on Mr. Farraday."

"He's rich. He's probably used to people staring at him."

"I don't think that anyone ever gets used to people staring at them and asking nosy questions. Besides, where he's from people probably don't make him feel like some sort of bug under a microscope. There are lots of rich people in Chicago. Lots of interesting cars, too."

"Oh, come on, Colleen. We're not going to bite him."

"No, you're going to bug him. The man just got home after being in the hospital, he's still recuperating and he wants some alone time with his son while they get used to each other. He doesn't need to become an oddity on display. And I don't want you asking him any questions about Lisa, either. I especially don't want you doing *that*, and after what I heard in town yesterday, I know that you will, so don't tell me otherwise. Rob, is that you? Don't you have a job?"

"It's my break time."

"Well, break time's over. Now, all of you go on back to town. Sooner or later Dillon will show up, and then and only then, if he wants, he'll answer your questions. The Applegate should be a sanctuary, though. Off-limits."

"You're a harsh woman, Colleen. And getting snootier every day. Why is that guy staying here, anyway? We all know how you feel about men on your place, and he's sure not a ranch hand."

"No, Harve, and neither am I. I'm the owner and

I call the shots, including who I invite here." Her point was clear. Dillon had been invited. They hadn't.

"Maybe you're trying to keep us away because you wouldn't mind getting engaged again, this time to a rich man who could spend his money on the Applegate and turn it into a moneymaker. If you keep him to yourself, no other woman can snatch him up the way it happened with Dave."

Intense silence met that comment, followed by some throat clearing and someone swearing beneath their breath. At that point, Dillon decided it was time to make an appearance. He slipped between the last of the trees, coming out just to the east of the entrance to the Applegate. His eyebrows rose. There were at least half a dozen cars jammed up at the entrance, all blocked by Colleen's pickup truck. She was standing in the bed, her blond curls fluttering in the breeze, and looking glorious in her obvious anger. Good. Because if someone had hurt her and brought her to tears, he'd just have to hit them and he wasn't in nearly good enough physical condition yet to dodge quickly if it came to that.

"I'm going to try to forget that you said that, Rob," Colleen said, but her voice seemed strained.

Dillon moved forward. He stared directly at Colleen, who looked startled, then started to the edge of the wagon bed. He shook his head.

"Hello, Colleen. I don't mean to interrupt this

meeting, but I was out taking a walk and it's sure a nice day, isn't it? You've got some great scenery here, too. I'm really glad I got out of Chicago to see it."

He turned to the men. "Hi, everyone. I'm Dillon Farraday."

There was some throat clearing, some shuffling. Some calling out of names. Harve Enson, Bill Winters, Rob Enson. More.

Dillon nodded. "I'm glad to make your acquaintance, but I couldn't help overhearing part of the conversation as I was walking through the orchard, and I think some things may need clearing up. For the record, Colleen has been the perfect hostess to me, and I've been a total pain of a guest," he said, using the hated word. "I dropped in on her out of the blue, and she's been caring for my baby for three months, which has to have cost her some work hours. In spite of that, she's made me feel welcome. So, while I really want to be a model visitor to your fine state and not make any unnecessary waves, I have to tell you that I would really take exception to anyone who criticized Colleen or embarrassed her or gave her any grief for taking Toby and me in. I'd definitely have to do something about that," Dillon said.

By now, everyone was looking at him. A small buzz of voices began in the crowd, and Colleen uttered something Dillon couldn't make out, but sounded like a muffled curse. She crossed her arms.

Dillon would have liked to have climbed up to stand in the back of the truck with her, but he didn't trust his leg to enable him to do that without him falling and looking like a fool. Right now, a commanding presence was called for.

"Well, now, Dillon, we all know better than to insult Colleen. She can ride a horse or shoot a gun better than any of us can," one older man said. "And when she was younger, she could beat up the boys if they messed with her. Rob here didn't mean anything by his comment. He was just irritated and not thinking straight. Nobody set out to insult Colleen, and they wouldn't. She's one of us."

"And I'm not," Dillon said with a smile.

The man looked startled. "I didn't mean it that way. I just meant...I meant that we all like Colleen. She's almost like one of the men."

Dillon frowned. Colleen was definitely nothing like a man, but since she didn't look happy to see him, and he had a distinct feeling that he'd already undermined some of her power simply by showing up here, he wasn't going to point out the fact that she was very obviously and achingly female. Or at least he wasn't going to point that out yet. That time might still come along.

"But I'm glad you showed up, Dillon, because

we wanted to meet you. Colleen, it looks like we win, after all," one of the men said.

Now Dillon was sure that he'd made a tactical error by showing up. He didn't care about the darn car or even about becoming a tourist attraction, but he did care about Colleen's pride.

"I *didn't* bring the car you wanted to see," he pointed out.

"But you'll let us see it, won't you? Most of us don't have the money to be allowed near enough to even test drive a car that costs well over a hundred grand. And based on your reaction to Rob's comment, I can see that you're a good guy," the man who appeared to be Harve said.

"I'm glad you think so. And I *will* bring the car into town…eventually. Right now Colleen and I have too much to do. No offense, but I need her right now worse than you need to see my car."

Some grumbling ensued. Dillon heard some man muttering that he had been talked into driving all the way out here for nothing and now had to drive all the way back home with no gossip to tell his wife. She wasn't going to be happy with him.

"What do you need Colleen for?" someone suddenly asked.

Dillon looked the man right in the eye. He could have simply laid the facts out in black and white. He wasn't the least bit ashamed that he had asked Colleen to tutor him in how to be a good dad, but the fact that all these men seemed to feel that it was their right to treat her as if she had no privacy...

"That's between me and Colleen," he said. "But I'll tell you this much. She's teaching me to be a better man. She deserves to be treated with respect. You need to back off from bothering her about me."

Colleen opened her mouth. She didn't look happy, but then she shook her head and shut her mouth.

"*We* need to go," she told him. She jumped down from the bed of the truck and climbed in.

Giving the men a nod, Dillon opened the passenger door and, using mostly his arms, leveraged himself smoothly into the vehicle.

Behind him, he could hear quiet conversation as the men returned to their trucks and cars. "Do you think they're dating?"

"No."

"Yes."

"No. Bill, the man was married to Lisa. Colleen's great, but she's a...I don't know what the term is nowadays, but she's a tomboy."

"He wasn't looking at her like she was a tomboy."

"Uh..."

Dillon couldn't catch the rest. Doors slammed, cars took off. He glanced to his left and saw that Colleen's color was high.

Interesting.

She headed off toward the house. "You shouldn't have done that."

"What?"

"Defended me. Come down to help me. Threatened to take action if someone insulted me."

"I didn't like their tone."

"I didn't, either, but they're mostly harmless. Most of this bunch is retired and they're bored. You're different and new and exciting. Something to see. Something to talk about."

"That doesn't excuse them trampling on your pride."

"I would have handled it. I'm used to handling it. I can hold my own."

"I didn't say you couldn't, but you came down here to protect me. I'm not letting you take risks for my sake, not when I'm perfectly capable of and used to taking my own risks."

Colleen stopped the truck.

"I know that, but…Dillon, I *have* to be in charge on the ranch. You're only here for a short while but I'm here forever. I'm responsible for lives—of people, of animals, of this whole operation. I'm responsible for everything that happens here. I can't be seen as weak and dependent on a man to step in and help me when things get tough."

Her tone, the memory of a few snippets of conversation, her comments about her stepfather, Rob's comments about her wanting to get engaged *again*, Millie's concerns about how people treated Colleen…

"Tell me…this hasn't always been a choice, has it? You've had to become strong, to establish yourself as unbending?"

Colleen stared at him through eyes that reflected old wounds, but her jaw was tight. "I've agreed to help you, I'm *glad* to be able to help you, but I'm not one of your employees or your soldiers. You can't simply command me to give up my secrets."

Because she was right, because his request might have been out of line and too personal and also because she looked petrified at the thought of telling him anything personal, guilt slipped through Dillon.

"You're totally right about that," he said.

"I have to stay in control. This ranch, everything that happens on it, it's personal to me. I just…my father…he loved this ranch. He died when I was young, and my mother was fragile and weak and ended up marrying a man who seemed strong but was merely mean and lazy. He and his son belittled me constantly, and she said nothing. He didn't let me do much other than work, except for the rodeo. That he allowed only because he felt it made him look good when I won.

"But I had one retreat. This ranch. My stepfather wasn't that interested in it other than letting it support him, and he was slowly leaching it of all its operating cash. Some of the older ranch hands who were still around taught me everything they knew, and this ranch became my sanctuary. Years later, when my mother and stepfather and step-brother died in a plane crash and the ranch became wholly mine, a man asked me to marry him, but when I found out that it was the ranch he wanted, not me, I broke things off. Almost immediately, he married another woman who gave him what he wanted. So, this is my world. I control it and everything that happens here. It's where I fit, and it's the other women's home, too. If I fail with it, they lose their home.

"So, I can't fail and I can't quit. Succeeding, however, means I have to be in charge of things. The buck stops here. Always."

"Meaning that having a man step in to protect you takes something away from you."

"Well, it *was* nice," she admitted. "I'm certainly not used to a man stepping up to defend me or threatening to protect my honor and reputation."

"Ouch. I sound like a domineering jerk."

"Maybe, more like a warrior."

"Colleen, I really am grateful to you for all you're doing for me and Toby, and…"

She looked over at him when he paused.

"There's something else I have to tell you. I don't really want to because I hate to worry you," he said. "I know how you feel about Toby."

Instantly, she sat up higher. "Is he sick? What's wrong?"

He shook his head. "He's fine. At least he was when I left. But Lisa...I think that Lisa is going to be a problem, one I'm going to have to address, like it or not. Considering the fact that she left him here, and she's already called you, you might get sucked in. I'll try to keep that from happening."

"Didn't I just tell you that you couldn't protect me? You know I'll help. Whatever I can do, I'll help you."

He reached out and traced his fingertips down the soft skin of her jaw. "And you said that *I* was a warrior. You just jump right in without any thought to your own welfare, don't you?"

She shrugged. "It's a bad habit, one that's gotten me in trouble from time to time."

"Maybe, but it's also incredibly appealing." He shouldn't be touching her. Ever. She was married to her ranch for better or worse. He had a life and a business in Chicago, and this...this flood of sensation she called up in him owed nothing to logic. Because logic told him that neither of them wanted a forever kind of relationship. It also told him that she would be hurt by anything less.

That left no outlet, no way forward, no way for him to touch her without guilt. Besides, he was *not* going to be another one of those men she'd known who hadn't cared about her feelings.

But suddenly she reached out and grasped the collar of his shirt in both hands. "You shouldn't say things like that," she whispered. Then she pulled him close for a quick, hard, mind-numbing kiss. A fantastic kiss that left his lips burning, his head spinning and his body craving more. Much more.

"We both wanted to do that, didn't we?" she asked when she pulled back just as fast as she'd started. There was uncertainty and a trace of vulnerability in her voice.

"Oh, yes, we did. Still do," he said with a grin.

She let her breath out. "Well, that's about all I can stand for today. I need to concentrate on work."

"You're the boss," he said as she put the truck in gear and headed back to the house. "You're in charge."

Which was good, because Dillon was beginning to think that he wasn't in charge of himself at all where Colleen was concerned.

CHAPTER SIX

COLLEEN felt as if she was having an out-of-body experience. Dillon made her too aware of herself in ways that she wasn't used to. That kiss…had she really kissed him? Just like that?

She had. The darn man just made her crazy with his insistence on treating her as if she was some kind of precious porcelain when everyone knew she was a tough woman. But that kiss. She'd been tempted beyond all belief to touch him, and when she had, the heat and emotions and desire that had slammed through her had been overwhelming. Too much. She hadn't known what to do about them. And she still didn't.

Well, no, that wasn't true. What she needed to do was ignore them. Sooner or later Dillon would leave.

In the meantime, she'd try to get back to doing what she did best. Taking care of business and people. As she'd told him, she'd already spent large portions of her life taking charge of others. Her stepfather had been a total jerk, but he'd been right about one or two things. Colleen had been awkward. She'd never been a girly girl.

But she *was* a fighter, one with a purpose. This ranch was her kingdom. And right now, something other than the too potent energy swirling between her and Dillon was disturbing her kingdom. And she was going to do something about it.

It was late. The bunkhouse had already gone dark, but she could still hear Dillon moving around. Going to the door leading out to the porch, she knocked.

He answered the door wearing a black T-shirt and jeans. She couldn't help noting the strength in his biceps, but she didn't want to notice that. It wasn't why she'd sought him out. "We should talk about Lisa," she said.

"Name the place."

Not here. He'd already pulled out his bed. They could sit in the kitchen, but the night was warm. The kitchen felt hot and sticky. He'd almost finished with the front porch today, but the swing still hadn't been hung.

"The picnic table in the yard will do. It's close enough that the monitor will pick up Toby if he wakes, but far enough from everyone else that no one will hear us. And it's out in the open."

He smiled at that.

She felt her face growing warm. "You're safe," she said, tipping her chin up. "I don't intend to jump you again."

"Did you think I was worried that you might?" he asked, raising one eyebrow.

She thought…no, she wasn't thinking straight at all right now.

"Let's go outside," she said.

He led the way. The stars had come out and stretched across the sky in a navy-and-white-spangled blanket that twinkled and glowed. Dillon held out his hand to help Colleen up onto the table and, without thought, she took it. His big fingers closed around hers, his warmth flowed into her. She breathed in deeply, trying to control her reaction, to slow the sparks that were zipping through her.

Concentrate, she told herself.

"Tell me about Lisa," she said. "I know her, but we weren't close. Mostly I remember Lisa as the star of Bright Creek, the girl every other girl seemed to want to be when we were growing up."

"Even you?"

"Not the way other girls did. I wouldn't have liked having that much attention turned on me. I was always awkward, as if my body was a bad fit. I still feel that way lots of times, except when I'm on a horse. But what I wanted doesn't matter. What does Lisa want? And how is that going to affect you and Toby?"

"I hope it won't affect us much at all. I'm hoping that we can just go on with our lives, but those aren't the vibes I'm getting from Lisa. And what I'm hearing about her doesn't bode well for Toby and me." He shook his head.

"Tell me," she said.

"I gave her a very generous settlement, more than what was required legally, but my sources tell me that she's running through it quickly and living beyond her means. Not an easy feat, but she appears to be doing it. The baby...she *never* expressed a desire for a baby. She left him with you with no way of reaching her but suddenly, as soon as I showed up here and met him, as soon as I fell for that cute little guy, she called me when she had never called before."

"You think Toby is a bargaining chip for more money?"

"I hope I'm wrong about that. And it's not that I'm worried about the money so much. It's how far she'll take this."

Colleen knew just what he meant. "When we were in school once, Esme Hawkins got a dress that was the prettiest I had ever seen. Esme had never had so much attention before in her life, I don't think. But when we were out playing at recess, Esme tripped over Lisa's foot and got her dress all dirty. It looked like an accident, Lisa didn't try to hide the fact that it had been her foot that had gotten in the way, and she apologized profusely. I wouldn't have thought anything of it at all, except the very next week Lisa came in wearing an equally pretty new dress. As if she had to prove a point and reclaim her title. Maybe it was a coincidence, but there were lots of those coincidences over the years. Nothing serious, just Lisa having to always be the one and only. Lisa flirting with the male teachers, complimenting the female teachers who were the toughest graders on their hair and nails and clothes. There was something about her that made even adults want to win her favor. But she is, as you've heard, the best in Bright Creek, so maybe I simply have a vivid imagination. I shouldn't be speculating when I have no proof."

She glanced up. Dillon was looking down at her, the moonlight shining in his eyes. "Did you have an experience similar to Esme's with Lisa?"

Colleen laughed. "No. Lisa liked me or at least she didn't bother me. I posed no threat to her crown whatsoever. I was interested only in books and broncs and the Applegate. Well, back then I was still interested in boys."

"And, of course, now you're not." He took her hand and rubbed his thumb across her palm.

She shivered and gave him a look. "Being interested and following through on being interested are two different things. I try to be smart."

"You *are* smart. You read people very well." He released her hand.

"Do you mean that your experience of Lisa was similar to mine?"

"No." He shook his head. "I wasn't entranced by Lisa at first. I was too focused on my work and my company. In some ways I was like Lisa."

"You wanted to be the center of attention?"

"I needed my company to succeed. When I was growing up, I had no anchor. My parents barely knew I existed half the time, and the nannies they hired came and went. I was untethered, adrift, combative and unhappy. I wanted structure, but there wasn't any. There was nothing and no one in my life to hold my attention until I discovered that the family business held the answers.

"Engineers can make the seemingly impossible possible. They can harness science and math and change life for the better. The company and what it stands for, a logical, well-ordered set of rules that, when applied, can create something that works to make the world a better place, gave me a sense of purpose and control when I was seriously adrift. It still does. I live by logic. My company represents a world that performs according to prescribed rules. Outcomes can be anticipated. Applying those kinds of rules with predictable outcomes is how I live my life, too. Letting my emotions control me when I was young had been disastrous for me when I finally faced the fact that my parents didn't care about me and never had. I didn't have a single soul who cared that I was even alive, and the dark feelings that followed that admission nearly destroyed me. I did risky, crazy things. I started down a path that would have ended in tragedy or prison if I hadn't had the good luck to have a run-in with a police officer who convinced me that my life *could* get much worse if I let it. Deciding to concentrate on my work and my duties was the solution that saved me. Unfortunately, with Lisa, who seemed like a sensible choice for a man like me, I read her wrong."

Colleen nodded. "Well, Lisa is a pretty good actress. People see what she wants them to see. And they're blinded by her beauty."

"I don't remember being blinded by beauty or an overwhelming passion. I had simply reached a time in my life when I wanted someone who would fit the part of my wife well and I didn't consider how we would fit *together*, I suppose."

She smiled. "Well, at least your initial decision sounds as if it was based on logic."

"What's happening now with her and Toby isn't. She left him and now she's calling, but without any obvious purpose. I don't know what she's planning, but I know that I won't let her use him. He's not a bargaining chip and if she intends to try to make him into one, I need to have a way of blocking her. Her desertion of him should carry some weight with a court if it comes to that, but…"

"But as I said, Lisa's a convincing actress," Colleen interjected. "In a custody battle, she might throw herself on the mercy of the court and claim a change of heart after she'd been apart from her child for a while. And she might win. So, you need a plan."

"A logical plan. One that makes sense and ups my odds of winning, because I don't intend to lose my son."

"Then you need to make a fantastic home for him. A haven. You need to show the world that he comes first with you, that you're focusing all your attention on providing a safe and secure environment."

Dillon smiled.

"Why are you looking at me that way?"

"That's what you've made here. A haven."

She shrugged. The moon was rising. Dillon looked like a beautiful man-god in the moonlight, his sharp male jawline shadowed, inviting the curve of her hand to rest there.

Look away, she told herself. Think of something else.

"You have a home in Chicago, don't you, where you could make a life with him?"

"I haven't been back there yet, and I gave the house to Lisa in the settlement. I'll need more than just bricks and mortar, though. I was raised in a huge house, but it wasn't a home."

"Still, it's a good place to start."

"Which is true. I'll begin looking for one tomorrow."

Good. And yet, that meant he would begin to think of leaving. Maybe even before the three weeks were up. He might have no choice. Colleen's heart clenched at the thought.

"That's very sensible," she said.

He took her hand. "This isn't." He kissed her palm, and butterflies did aerial dives in her stomach. "Thank you for giving me some direction, a calm, reasonable approach. You should come to bed," he said, standing up. "It's late."

She hesitated.

"I meant come inside and go to your own bed, Colleen," he stressed. "I wasn't trying to seduce you, much as I'd like to."

"I'll come inside. Soon," she promised. And she watched him walk away from her. What were the words he'd used? Calm and reasonable? She only wished she felt that way, because Dillon made her feel a million things, but none of them were either calm or reasonable.

CHAPTER SEVEN

DILLON knew the minute Colleen came in the door an hour later. He couldn't fall asleep until she came inside. In spite of the fact that she'd lived here all her life, in spite of the fact that they were miles from anywhere with no threats in sight, he needed to know she was safe before he would allow himself to rest. And even once she came inside, he didn't rest easily. The memory of her sitting in the dark beside him with the stars overhead haunted him. Had he turned just a bit he could have drawn her into his arms.

What if he had kissed her and taken it further than mere kisses?

"Then you'd have to shoot yourself, because you would hurt her," he muttered. The last thing she needed was a transient man trooping into her life, messing with her emotions and then heading out of town. Wasn't he already mad at the men who had used and abused her in the past? Did he really want to join their ranks?

Keep it simple, Farraday, he told himself. Just do what needs doing.

She had made a helpful suggestion about the house. And it was a good way to keep his mind on something other than touching Colleen.

So, the next day when he had finished putting the last touches on her porch, he called a Realtor in Chicago.

Three days later, he had an entire folder of information, but he still didn't know what he wanted and needed, because he'd never been a father before. So, when lunchtime rolled around, he tracked down all the women and asked if they would give him their expert advice.

"You want our help?" Colleen asked.

"I trust your judgment."

"Sounds good to me. I love looking at houses," Millie said.

"Oh, yeah. And in this case, with money no object, it's like pretending you really can have all the cool things you would, in reality, never be able to afford in real life," Gretchen said.

"Do you have any specific considerations, features you'd like?" Colleen asked.

"I was hoping all of you could help me draw up a master list of what would be the perfect house for a grown man and a baby, if such a house even exists. Then we'll go from there."

He and Colleen exchanged a look. He knew

that this ranch house, even with all the work it needed, was the perfect house for *her*.

"Okay, I'll bite," Julie said. "It's obvious that, since money is no object—I take it that it isn't—that you should have lots of space. There will be sleepovers, eventually, you know. Gretchen and I once got to have a sleepover when Mom was still alive. I'll never forget that we stayed up all night watching princess-themed movies. It was fantastic."

"It was," Gretchen said. "We had everyone bring stuffed animals and we put on a play. That was before daddy burned all our things to punish us."

"Oh, sweetie," Colleen said and gave Gretchen a hug. Gretchen hugged her back and then Julie joined in.

Dillon looked as if he wanted to punch someone. "I don't mean to denigrate your family," he told the women, "but some men don't deserve to have children. I'm sorry you had to go through that."

"I'm just glad Toby has a father like you," Julie said. "Toby's never going to have to feel scared. He won't have to give up his childhood because his father's a jerk."

But, of course, Colleen thought, Toby's mother wasn't as nice as Dillon. Dillon had to win. And Lisa had a habit of hitting below the belt. They had to make Dillon's case as tight as possible and he had to present as the perfect father providing the perfect home.

"Gretchen, what do you think would help?" she asked.

"I'd vote for a big yard with room for a play-ground," Gretchen said. "A garden with flowers. Even guys love flowers, even if they won't always admit it. And there should be at least one tree with some branches that are low enough for a kid to get a leg up when he climbs. If it's got a nice crook where a tree house could be located, so much the better."

"And a big kitchen," Millie added. "Boys eat a lot. Or my sons did when they were growing up. Besides, you'll probably have birthday parties. You'll need space."

Dillon smiled. He looked over the women's heads to Colleen, who hadn't joined in yet. It was obvious that her ranch-hand friends were getting in the spirit of things.

More suggestions flew. A playroom. A theater. A library. A basketball court. The list was growing so long Dillon knew it wouldn't be possible to include everything. But the women had moved beyond their sad memories. They were having fun and so was he.

But when someone suggested a good staircase to slide down, Colleen looked into Dillon's eyes. She stood up and walked over to him. "Make it

safe," she said. "That will be important. And...
make sure it's the house that *you* want. The kind
of place you'll want to come home to every night,
one that feels like a comfortable fit. You'll be living
there, too, you know. What's most important in a
house to you?"

Dillon stared down into Colleen's face. He was
close enough to touch her, but of course he
wouldn't, not with everyone here. What was most
important in a house to him?

A big bed. He nearly groaned. Had he really
thought that? He hadn't said it out loud, had he?

Looking around, he could see he hadn't. The
women were still waiting for him to answer.

"A house with a sturdy front porch," he said,
"and an enclosed back porch with a top-of-the-line
sleeper sofa."

Laughter greeted his comment, but Colleen
wrinkled her nose. "All right, you can buy a new
one. The one you want. As long as you take it with
you when you go. It will be yours."

Despite his good intentions, he reached out and
touched her face. "I was kidding, not complain-
ing."

"I know. But it *is* an awful mattress."

"Why? Have you tried it lately, Colleen?"
Gretchen asked, and he turned to see that she was
teasing, but also wide-eyed with curiosity.

"Gretchen," Colleen warned.

"I'm afraid I'm the sole occupant of the killer sofa bed," he said, winking.

"I think you just like to complain about it to make me feel guilty," Colleen said in a teasing tone.

Everyone laughed again, and Dillon realized that he felt at home in this group of women. Too much at home. That wasn't good. He couldn't start doing stupid things now. Getting emotionally wrapped into this group, or especially into Colleen, would only end in disaster for both of them. She had her base and her sanctuary. He had his. She had obligations. His were different. There was no middle ground, and she didn't want a man. The Applegate was and might always be "no males" territory. He and Toby had simply been granted temporary sanctuary.

As if he knew that his father was thinking about him, the baby, who was cuddled up against Millie, began to babble.

"What's that, Toby? You think your dad is right about that sofa bed?" Dillon asked.

Colleen wrinkled her nose. "Don't you go putting words in my baby's mouth."

And just like that, the atmosphere changed.

"I meant *your* baby, of course," Colleen said.

"Don't be sad, Colleen," Millie said. "I'm sure that when he takes Toby back to Chicago he'll call. He'll make sure that Toby stays in touch over the years, won't you, Dillon?"

Before he had a time to open his mouth, to breathe, to think, Colleen held up her hand. "Do not answer that," she said. Which was good because he didn't know how to answer. He knew that maintaining contact with a woman who drove him insane with desire but to who he could never make love or marry would be a kind of hell.

"And don't any of you make Dillon feel guilty about Toby," she said to her friends.

"Of course we wouldn't, Colleen," Julie said. "It isn't Dillon's fault that you can't have a baby of your own."

And that was when the chandelier fell on their heads. Metaphorically, anyway, Dillon thought later.

For a long moment time seemed to stop. No one breathed. No one spoke. Even the clock on the wall seemed to stop ticking.

"You didn't know," Millie said to Dillon.

"Why should he? It isn't exactly the kind of thing I was just going to drop into a conversation over lunch. And besides, there was no reason for Dillon to know. It was an accident I had *years* ago. It's not his fault I can't have a child, and there's nothing he can do about it."

She turned to Dillon and pasted on a smile. It was totally phony. He knew it. She knew he knew it. But what she was telling him was that she didn't want to talk about it. How could he not honor that when the topic was one that was so painful for her?

And Toby was starting to fret, to twist in Millie's arms and whimper, as if he was absorbing the charged atmosphere and was frightened.

Automatically, as if she'd done it a thousand times and probably had, Colleen turned to the baby, a look of love and concern on her face. Quickly she moved toward him, but then she stopped suddenly just two feet from Toby, who was waving his little hands in distress.

Colleen looked suddenly smaller, her shoulders more rounded, her head dropped slightly.

She turned away from Toby and looked at Dillon. "You need to hold your son," she said. "Now, I'd better get some work done." She smiled sadly. Then she quietly left the room.

As Dillon cuddled his child he realized that something elemental had happened here. Colleen had decided that it was time to start letting go. She would begin to transfer the care of Toby to him in earnest.

And she would begin to back out of the picture.

This should have been a moment of pride for Dillon, the fact that she trusted him enough to turn control of Toby over to him.

Instead, when he heard the front door open and close a few seconds later, he simply wanted to go after her, stop her, wherever she was going.

In fact, he must have made a move toward the door, because he felt a hand on his sleeve. Millie was shaking her head.

"She'll probably be working all night in her shop."

When he frowned in confusion, Millie smiled. "I guess she didn't tell you. Colleen's an artist." She gestured toward the beautiful decorated glass vases that were in every room in the house. "The wind chimes, the sculpture...that, more than anything, has kept this ranch going when times got rough. Colleen can't create a child, but she creates beautiful things nonetheless."

"I didn't know," he said. It occurred to him that there were lots of things he didn't know about Colleen.

Things he wanted to know but never would. As he left the room and headed toward the nursery with Toby, he reached up and touched one of the chimes that hung in the doorway. Its soft sounds were like music. Sad but very sweet and very beautiful.

Just like the woman responsible for them.

Colleen didn't spend all night in her workshop. In fact, she had done very little work when she put her tools down and faced the facts. She had behaved badly, stealing the happiness from what had been a fun afternoon.

Dillon was buying a house for him and Toby, she and her friends had been given the honor of helping him decide how to make things special for them and she had walked out just when things had come to fruition. It wasn't as if she hadn't spent years living with the knowledge that she couldn't produce a child.

No, her sudden sadness had been because the house represented the beginning of the end. Dillon would be leaving soon. Not that that was a surprise exactly, but she hadn't expected that sharp pain that had hit her when she'd realized how fast time was flying. She'd just had to get away.

And now you have to go back, she told herself. *The man probably thinks you're acting crazy or that you're rolling in self-pity.* Which she was…a little bit. And that just wasn't going to continue. She was not that kind of woman.

"So, suck it up, Applegate," she told herself. "And go help the man do what he needs to do."

She opened the door to the house quietly. The curtains were open in the bunkhouse, and she could see Millie reading by the window, so Colleen knew that only Toby and Dillon were in the house.

She went directly to Toby's room, but no one was there. Then she heard a low baby gurgle.

And then a deep male voice mimicking the gurgle. "Oh, you are so talented, buddy," Dillon said. "That's a tough sound to make. How about this one?" He made a buzzing sound like a bee.

Colleen poked her head around the door. Dillon

was sitting on a blanket holding Toby in front of him. Toby was studying his daddy very solemnly with those big blue eyes.

"No? Not that sound? Okay, about this one?" He leaned forward and very gently made a raspberry noise against Toby's tiny tummy. The baby's eyes got big and round and then he squealed and grabbed a handful of Dillon's hair.

"You little squirt," Dillon said, disentangling himself and smiling at his son. "You are going to be trouble when you grow up, you know that? And I'm going to love you no matter what."

Toby blew a bubble. He smiled.

It was a beautiful thing to see, this big man and this tiny baby enjoying each other's company. Then she realized that she was snooping. She hadn't even announced her presence.

"You're going to get a stiff neck sticking your head around corners that way," Dillon said, making her jump and squeal almost as loud as Toby had.

She came all the way into the room. "I didn't mean to keep my presence a secret and I wasn't spying," she protested. "Well, maybe just a little."

"Uh-oh, Toby. I wonder how much of our conversation she heard. She probably knows our secrets now. We may have to tie her up and hold her prisoner."

Toby's eyes followed every movement of his father's head and mouth. He made a very small grunt.

"Toby says we must show lenience to the princess who has sheltered us and given us asylum." Dillon put his hand in front of his face to block his mouth and spoke to Colleen in an aside. "My son has a heart of gold, it seems, but I was kind of looking forward to having you as my prisoner," he teased.

"Toby, pay no attention to your daddy's antics. He's crazy." She leaned closer and smiled at the baby, who gifted her with one of his most beatific smiles.

"You're an angel, sweetie," she told him, "but it looks as if you're wearing part of your dinner." Milk had dribbled down his neck.

"A slight incident with the bottle," Dillon told her. "I was just going to give him a bath. We were just waiting."

"For what?"

"A how-to session," he said. "It occurred to me that reading your instructions on how to give a baby a bath while in the midst of actually carrying out those instructions might be tricky, given all the water and soap and slippery baby and instruction sheets. What if I smudge the paper and can't figure out what to do next?" His smile was huge, his teasing tone was seductive.

She reached out and placed her hand on his jaw. "You don't have to do this, you know."

This time he didn't smile and he turned into her

hand slightly, his beard scratching a bit. She loved the sensation. Her heart did a flip. "Don't have to what?" he asked. "Give the baby a bath?" His voice echoed through her body right down to her toes.

She shook her head slowly. "You don't have to be careful with me. You don't have to make me laugh, although I like laughing with you. You don't have to shy away from the difficult topics. I can't have a baby. You know it. I know it. We've said it out loud, and that's not a problem. I'm not made of glass. Okay?"

"Not glass. Flesh and bone and…I'm sorry. I just can't ignore the fact that you've been hurt, Colleen."

"You can't change it, either. I know that all too well. It was a freak riding accident where I ended up cut up. When the doctors told me that I'd never have children, it stunned me at first, that riding—something I love so much—could take the thing I most wanted. I got angry, and I hated the fact that I was broken when I'd never let anything break me before. So, I got back on my horse and spent a lot of time riding the range and screaming at the sky that first year. I channeled my anger into my racing, but finally I realized that I could fight and yell all my life and it wouldn't change a thing. So, I put it behind me—mostly—and I need you to put it out of your mind, too. I would hate it if you pitied me or were careful with me because of this. So, Dillon…don't be careful."

For several seconds, tension filled the air as he stared at her, studied her.

"Dillon, I mean it."

He muttered a curse and looked to one side.

"Dillon?"

He swung his head around, his eyes dark and fierce. "All right."

She frowned. "That could mean a lot of things."

"In this case," he said quietly, "it means I won't be…careful."

Which sounded so much more dangerous than he probably meant it to, Colleen was sure. She nodded and managed a shaky smile. "So, okay, yes," she said, determined to change the subject and the mood. "I'll show you how to give a baby a bath. It's not difficult. You just have to make sure to put everything out that you need ahead of time, because you can never leave him alone in the tub. I'll show you how to make sure the temperature of the water is right. And I just know you're going to be a whiz at this. Because you like to talk and tease. And Toby likes to listen to people talk and tease while he takes a bath."

"Ah, another one of those teacher-type pats on the back," he said, allowing her to move beyond the "Colleen can't have babies" topic. "I'm starting to like those."

And because she was starting to like a lot of things about Dillon, far too much, Colleen made herself get right to the task. Dillon talked to his son the whole time he was cleaning him up, but the excitement of having his two favorite people to himself at the same time was clearly too much. His arms flailed more than usual, and by the time they were through, both Colleen and Dillon had generous splashes of water dotting their clothes. Toby, of course, was adorable and dry in his little towel with the hood.

"Thank you for the lesson. I think I've got the hang of it now, but you'd better go put on something dry."

"Oh, I'm okay," she said. "I can handle a little water."

"Maybe so, but I'm not sure that I can, or that I can be trusted," Dillon said, looking pointedly at her shirt where, she realized as she looked down, the outline of her bra was visible through the damp cloth.

Her eyes opened wide. She crossed her arms over her chest. "You," she said to Toby, "need to learn to bathe with more decorum and less splashing. You've embarrassed your daddy." And she leaned forward and kissed the baby's forehead. "Excuse me. I'll just take your advice and go put on something dry, change the scenery," she told Dillon.

He smiled and leaned forward and kissed her

right beneath the ear. "The scenery is beautiful. It's the observer who isn't sure he won't reach out and grab, given the chance. Not that I'm saying I would have gotten the chance or anything, mind you."

"You'll never know now, will you?" she teased as she left the room.

"That thing she told you about not splashing?" she heard Dillon say to Toby. "Don't listen. Splashing is fun, although that may be totally a guy thing. That's us, buddy. You and me. We're guys. Colleen, now, she's a woman. A beautiful woman," he clarified. "Especially beautiful after bathtime."

Colleen blushed all the way to her room. And in the middle of the night, she woke up, remembered Dillon's comment and blushed some more. She definitely needed to start pulling away or at least to work harder about not getting too close.

Think of staying away from Dillon as just another ranch chore, a goal, she told herself. *Something you just need to do.* But when she closed her eyes, she felt his mouth on hers, and her goals…she couldn't even remember what they were.

CHAPTER EIGHT

FIVE days later, the tension climbed a little higher, but this was nothing like the tension caused by her reactions to Dillon, Colleen thought as she hung up the phone and reviewed the conversation that had just transpired.

She had been meaning to call Lisa back ever since that first day when her phone had rung. Despite her anger at Lisa leaving Toby, a part of her had hoped that the woman had had some sort of valid reason. But what kind of valid reason could there be for abandoning your child and leaving no forwarding address…or not telling your husband or even your ex-husband that you were expecting his child until you had already delivered the baby?

So, despite the fact that the number had been on her phone's call log, she had put off contacting Lisa. Given the order of things, Lisa had probably simply been trying to reach Dillon, anyway. And she had already done so. At least that was what

Colleen had told herself…until the phone call from Lisa this morning.

"I hear that Dillon is staying at your ranch," Lisa had said.

Colleen took a deep breath and considered her words carefully. She knew that Dillon hadn't mentioned that fact in his phone call with Lisa. "I assume you've spoken to someone in town."

"I still have a few contacts there, yes. They don't know everything, though. So, why is he there?"

For some reason Colleen didn't want to tell Lisa that Dillon was taking lessons in parenting. If he wanted her to know that, he'd tell her. Besides, Colleen was afraid to tell her. Lisa was Toby's mother. She had rights, and one of those rights was to come ask for her baby back. There was no law stopping her. If someone else had something she no longer had, if Toby's value increased because Dillon wanted him, she might decide she wanted Toby, too.

"Dillon's a guest," Colleen said noncommittally.

"The Applegate never was a guest ranch."

Colleen could have told Lisa that it still wasn't, but that would only call up more questions. "I'm always adding new sidelines to the Applegate. Horses are expensive to keep."

"But Dillon is your only guest. If there had been others, Bill would have told me."

Colleen frowned. So Bill Winters was the one

spilling his guts to Lisa. Not a surprise, since he'd always wanted to date her.

"How long do you think he's going to stay there?"

Probably not long, but…

"I have no idea," Colleen said, but she was wondering why Lisa hadn't asked one question about Toby.

"How's the baby?" Lisa asked, as if she'd read Colleen's mind.

Perfect. Adorable. A total love. How could you leave him that way? Colleen thought. "He's doing well," she said.

"I can't come get him just yet," Lisa said. "Maybe when my situation changes." Which made Colleen's blood turn cold. If Dillon's contacts were right, Lisa was partying hard in Europe, not worrying about her baby. But, when she wanted something—if she should ever decide she wanted Toby—Colleen had no question that Lisa could "change her situation" at will, play the part of remorseful mother and play it convincingly enough to fool a judge who was in charge of determining the terms of custody.

"Let me offer a friendly word of warning," Lisa suddenly said. "Dillon's an attractive man and a wealthy one, but he's also used to calling the shots. He isn't easy to handle, even for someone who's experienced and knows how to handle men. I know you don't have that kind of experience, Colleen. I know a lot. I would be careful around Dillon if I were you."

Colleen felt as if bands of fear and indignation were squeezing her heart. "It's nice of you to worry about me, Lisa."

At that moment, Dillon walked in the door. Those bands closed tighter. And on the other end of the line, Lisa was laughing. It sounded like light laughter, but Colleen thought she heard a hard edge to it. Or maybe that was just her imagination because she was afraid Lisa would someday try to reclaim Toby on one of those whims she and Dillon had discussed.

Lisa, Colleen mouthed to Dillon.

"Of course I worry about you, Colleen," Lisa said. "No one knows better than I do that I took advantage of your kindness, but I'd hate to see you hurt by Dillon. And you will get hurt if you start thinking of him romantically. But then, you've never really been the romantic sort, have you?"

"No, I'm not romantic. You don't have to worry about me falling in love with Dillon," Colleen said, and she knew that her words were as much to reassure herself and Dillon as they were to stop Lisa from any more warnings.

"Good. I was really concerned for you when Bill told me that. Since you're taking care of Toby, I feel kind of protective toward you, and if I thought you were in danger of getting your heart broken by Dillon, I'd feel responsible. After all, he would never even be there if not for me. Maybe I should have left Toby with someone older, but you seemed like the right person at the time."

Colleen felt anger rising in her. She felt threatened, and she wanted nothing more than to tell Lisa off, but there was Toby and there was Dillon. Both of them would suffer if Lisa decided to…act like Lisa. Colleen couldn't do anything that would incite her to get angry and take action.

"Well, I really appreciate that, Lisa. I do," Colleen lied. "And, thank you again. But I really have to go now. A ranch takes a lot of time and effort and I have a foal that desperately needs tending to. I'm sure we can talk more later."

She hung up without letting Lisa even say goodbye.

If Dillon hadn't been standing there, Colleen would have pressed her hands against her heart. She would have leaned over, put her hands on her knees and taken deep breaths to keep from getting dizzy. She had hung up on Lisa Farraday, who had the power to harm Dillon and Toby.

"What did she want?" Dillon asked.

What could she say? He had been there when she made that declaration about not falling in love with him.

Colleen turned to him. "I think she wanted to

make sure I wasn't poaching what she still thinks of as hers. I think I just became Esme Hawkins and you're the pretty dress."

Dillon looked unconvinced. "You're forgetting that Lisa was the one who divorced *me*."

No, she wasn't forgetting that. If Lisa hadn't divorced Dillon, the two of them would still be married. Colleen hadn't forgotten that. And wouldn't. But that wasn't what he was trying to say.

"Lisa may not be married to you anymore, but this is her town and her territory, and she is, as I mentioned, still the queen here. That means no one takes her place. Even if she divorced you, that may have just been the impetuous, scorned woman reacting. She probably didn't like it that you put your work before her pleasure, so she was punishing you. Knowing Lisa, she probably assumed she could come back and remarry you whenever she wanted, and you'd go along with that the way other men have. She'd have more power over you, because you would have learned your lesson. That's pure speculation based on her past performance, of course, but no matter what, she wouldn't want someone from here to waltz in and take what was once hers. And I…I think she may have threatened me. I definitely hung up on her. That's not good."

"Are you afraid of her?"

Colleen examined that statement. "Not for me."

Lisa couldn't take anything from her, Colleen realized, because she didn't *really* have anything Lisa wanted. "But for you and Toby—I don't want to antagonize her. She could make things difficult for you."

"Regarding custody."

"Yes."

"I've thought of that. I'm hoping we can reach an amicable arrangement."

They stared at each other for a long time. "What kind of arrangement do you want?" she asked.

"One where I get him all the time."

"You don't want to have to go to court over this."

"If what you say is true, and I believe it may be, then no. I like situations where I control all the variables. But, in the event that I might have to go to court—and it could come to that—I want to hold as many of the cards as I can."

"You need to demonstrate that you're the perfect dad." In Colleen's eyes, he was already that. But she wasn't a judge.

"I don't want to leave even one stone unturned."

She nodded. "Then we'd better consider all the possibilities, we'd better make sure you're as knowledgeable about raising a child as we can make you and we'd better make sure we cover all the bases and get you into the perfect setup back in Chicago as soon as possible."

Dillon suddenly smiled at her, and her heart did a triple somersault. "You are an amazing woman," he said. "You deserve an award, national recognition, a plaque and a spot on television about women who have made a difference. You're certainly being a tremendous help to me and Toby."

How could a woman not fall in love with a man who said things like that? Colleen wondered, then immediately regretted the thought. *She* couldn't fall in love with him. For so many reasons, ranging from the fact that Lisa would punish him if she thought that Colleen was showing an interest to the fact that Dillon really would break her heart to the fact that they lived in different worlds and different lifestyles a thousand miles apart. And both of them were committed to those worlds and those lifestyles. Her place was here. She mattered *here*. What was a woman supposed to do?

"Thank you," she said, doing the simple thing. "Now, I really should get some work done. I'd call Bill Winters and give him a piece of my mind for reporting on me and you to Lisa but he'd probably just tell her that I threatened him."

"I wouldn't worry about the man," Dillon said.

"Dillon, you can't do anything that would make you look…I don't know…violent at a time like this."

He shook his head. "I wouldn't do anything that would cause a problem." Which meant he probably still had some sort of plan.

Colleen looked at him and saw the warrior, the man who dealt in solutions. She could have told him to leave things alone completely, but...

"Who's worried?" she lied with a smile. "Everything here is just perfect."

Except for the fact that she kept wanting to kiss Dillon Farraday, everything was just fine.

"I mean it, Colleen," Dillon said. And just like that, he moved forward, looped his arm around her waist and pulled her so close that their mouths were almost touching. "Leave Bill to me. You're not to get hurt on my account."

"I won't," she lied.

"And I heard what you said about falling in love with me. We may not be in danger of that, but there's this," he said, kissing her so that it was all she could do not to wrap her arms around his neck and hang on. "It's a problem."

"I know."

"I like kissing you too much."

"I like kissing you, too. Too much. And I don't like it one bit. It's not smart and it's only going to cause trouble."

"Agreed. I'm going to have to work on self-control."

"You let me know how that works out," she said.

He smiled at her as he let her go. "So far it's not working at all."

"We'll keep trying." And somehow she managed

to walk away on legs that shook. Somehow she kept going and didn't look back.

Until she did.

He was still looking at her. Her body turned to flame. It was going to be a very hot afternoon, she thought as she attempted to get back to whatever it was she really needed to do on the ranch.

What *did* she need to do, anyway?

Kiss Dillon, her misbehaving brain told her.

Two days had passed. Toby was fretting because he'd been awakened unexpectedly from his nap when a branch had fallen on the roof. Dillon felt like fretting, too, but it had nothing to do with the branch. He was still brooding over that kissing conversation he'd had with Colleen. The self-control plan was not working real well.

But that wasn't his son's problem. "It's tough waking up from a nap, isn't it, buddy?" he asked, cuddling his son. "It's tough when you want something you can't have, too, isn't it?" He moved away from the table they were sitting next to so that Toby couldn't reach the sugar bowl he'd been trying to touch. "Like Colleen. We both like her, don't we?"

Toby gurgled.

"I'll take that as a yes."

His son let out a crowing sound.

"Okay, a really big yes. But neither of us can have her. She's got this ranch and...heck, she *needs* this ranch and everything that goes with it. She's got plans. Big plans, ones that don't involve men. Plans that involve staying here and running a ranch with her friends and setting up that camp to teach needy city girls how to ride and ranch. Can't do that in Chicago. Besides, she likes us well enough now, but she likes us partly because we're temporary, you know. She doesn't want to get tied to a man and, well, heck, you and I have plans, too. We've got things we need to do and all of those require being in Chicago. So, we're just going to have to get used to doing without her even if she's helping us a lot, you know?"

He cuddled Toby to him and dropped a kiss on the top of his head. And one of his son's little hands latched on to his shirt. Something about that just choked Dillon up. That trust. Those tiny fingers. He wanted...he wanted to call Colleen inside and show her, to tell her how it made him feel. But it was probably best to keep his distance from Colleen for a while. Kissing her was getting to be a habit, and the truth was that he wanted to do a lot more than kiss her.

That could only complicate things for both of them, and when he left here he didn't want him and his son to be something she would regret.

"It's just you and me, Toby," he said. But just then Toby bucked a bit and kicked his toe into the table. He let out a howl and then a sob that turned into more heartbreaking sobs. His little body shook. He was inconsolable and so was Dillon.

Looking at the little red dent on his baby's leg, he wanted to swear. He had let his son get hurt. Surely Colleen wouldn't have done that. Of course she wouldn't have.

Toby was snuffling and crying, and Dillon got to his feet. He walked out the door with Toby's little body cuddled up against him.

The movement seemed to do the trick, and Toby's cries died down to whimpers.

"Dillon, is everything all right?"

Dillon looked up and found himself standing just outside the corral where Colleen was mounted on a frisky palomino. She looked beautiful up there. She looked right.

"Darn it, I let him get hurt. He kicked into the table and now he has a red mark."

Dillon slid his palm under Toby's leg and showed Colleen.

Immediately the worried look in those big brown eyes disappeared and she smiled. "I can almost see it," she said.

From her attitude, Dillon knew that he had over-reacted. "Toby, she's making light of our situation. Two clueless guys in obvious need of direction. We're new at this. Doesn't she know that?" he asked, whispering the words against the top of Toby's head, loud enough for Colleen to hear.

Of course, she *did* know. "Looks like you need Dr. Colleen to look at that wound," she teased. "Just let me take Suzie's saddle off and go wash up."

By now Toby wasn't crying at all and Dillon wasn't worried anymore, but he had come to a decision within the past hour. He needed to talk to Colleen about it.

So, when she came back out, he smiled at her. "Let's walk."

She gave him a questioning look. "You look serious. I'm sure Toby is fine. Babies get little bumps and bruises all the time. You can't blame yourself."

"I don't take my responsibilities lightly, so yes, I can, but Toby's leg isn't what I want to talk about. It's a gorgeous day. Show me what I haven't seen."

To her credit, Colleen didn't mention his leg. Good. He hadn't been using his cane around the house much lately and he had decided to stop using it altogether, because holding a cane and a baby was just not practical. Still, it was probably going to give him trouble or at least ache for a good long time. Too bad. He had no intention of letting that stop him. Especially not now. Just when he was trying to prove that he was the perfect person to keep Toby full-time was no time to appear weak.

Colleen merely gave a curt nod and fell into step beside him, not saying anything. They passed another one of those wild and beautiful glass-and-metal sculptures similar to the one Dillon had seen in the orchard that day. "You're talented," he said. "I know people in Chicago who would pay a lot of money for something like that. How long have you been an artist?"

She looked a bit self-conscious when he glanced at her. "I'm not exactly an artist. I'm a reactionary. I started working with glass back when my stepfather and stepbrother were here. They liked to shoot guns when they were drunk, and they preferred shooting things that were made of glass. It didn't matter if it was expensive or pretty or meaningful. Just as long as it shattered in a satisfying way. I hated that. Not the shooting so much, but the indiscriminate drunkenness of it all. They tended to be that way about everything, and of course, they never cleaned up the glass, so if someone didn't do it, I had to. We had more animals then, and I didn't want them to get hurt. So, to funnel my anger and frustration, I started making things out of the glass. After a while it became a hobby and even after they were gone, I kept it up. Nowadays, I get the satisfaction of breaking the glass myself, so when I'm angry or frustrated, I tend to disappear into my workshop," she said, waving toward a small building.

It wasn't exactly the most perfect building Dillon had ever seen, and Colleen seemed to know what he was thinking.

"I know what it looks like," she said, "but this is one building I don't want you to touch. If it were dangerous, I would have got it fixed, but as it is, I like the slightly misshapen structure. It's unpolished and a bit rough."

"I know you well enough by now to realize that that's how you think of yourself. You identify with it."

She hesitated. "I've bonded with it, yes. It has significance to me. It reminds me that I fit here, that I'm a part of all this, rooted here, and that I can never stop trying to make things better. I owe it to the women who live and work here and the ones who will visit one day and hopefully take something meaningful and empowering away if I ever get the camp going. And if any of those girls end up needing an escape hatch, this place needs to be there for them. A rock, a safe place."

More than ever, Dillon understood the significance of this ranch she thought of as her sanctuary. She had to be here to take in lost lambs, those who had been mistreated.

"Toby and I are going to have to leave soon," he said suddenly. "We can't stay much longer."

Colleen stumbled and Dillon reached out one hand to catch her, but she shook her head and quickly righted herself. "Of course. Lisa has called too many times. There's something going on. You'll want to have all your chessmen in position should she decide to challenge your rights as a father."

And he also wanted to make sure that he got out before Colleen started meaning too much to him.

"That's about the gist of it," he said. "I've got the Realtor looking for the house. As soon as she finds one that fits, I want to furnish it, find someone to help me take care of Toby while I'm working and then I want to firmly establish the two of us in that stronghold. There can't be any question that I'm putting his welfare first or that I know what I'm doing."

She stopped. They had made it to the creek, upstream from where the fisherman were, but Dillon could hear them in the distance. "I can't imagine that anyone who knew you would question your dedication to him. Just…Dillon, look at the two of you," she said, biting her lip. When she looked up into his eyes, her own were misting up.

"You've done this for us," he said.

"No." She shook her head. "No one knows better than me that fathers have to actually *want* to be fathers in order for things to work out. This is all you."

Anger that she should have been denied what should have been rightfully hers, that any man should fail to see her value, surged through Dillon, but he could see that she was vulnerable right now.

And she was a woman who wanted to be and needed to be strong. She *was* strong, and she wouldn't want him to point out her moment of vulnerability any more than he liked having his weak leg pointed out.

Moreover, he was beginning to think that it would hurt her as much as it would hurt him if he didn't get to have Toby full-time. She'd dedicated herself to helping him. He couldn't let her or Toby or himself down.

"Before I leave, I want you to drill me, to teach me, to quiz me, so that I know at least some of what I should do in any given situation. Most people learn as they go, but with Lisa possibly plotting something, I don't feel I have that luxury."

"We'll burn the midnight oil," she promised. "We'll search the Internet and read all the books. We'll role-play. I promise we'll do all we can. We…all of us care. About Toby."

He stared into her eyes, and he burned to touch her.

Then he *was* touching her, but gently this time, pulling her close enough so that Toby was snuggled high up on his shoulder, his little hands touching both of them, connecting them. "I know you care," he said. "We're never going to forget what you've done for us, you know."

For long seconds they just stayed that way, together. Almost like a family, but…not. Then

Dillon felt her take a deep breath. She straightened. "We'd better get started. I'm going to tell you everything I've noticed about Toby that you may not have absorbed yet. Lisa will have the mantle of motherhood to bruit about, but you'll have the details of who your son actually is."

The fact that she'd thought of that, the fact that *she* knew those details and that she was willing to help him in this way…Dillon's chest hurt.

That couldn't matter. "Let's do it," he said. "If what my Realtor tells me is true, we might not have much more than a week, because as soon as the right place comes up, we're there. It won't be quite the three weeks I told you, but—"

"I know," she said. "You have to do it. You have to go."

CHAPTER NINE

IN FACT, Dillon had less than a week remaining. The next morning began with a gloomy sky and even gloomier news that one of his company's projects was in trouble, but his project manager had to leave town next week to tend to important family business. Dillon's presence was needed as soon as possible. He had spent the evening studying all the notes Colleen had given him and as many of the books and articles as they could lay their hands on. He could probably recite information that many pediatricians didn't know, he had the number of the Illinois Poison Center memorized in case of an emergency and he knew all the best medical Web sites and parenting resources.

But this morning, because of Farraday Engineering's problems, he'd been holed up with a telephone and computer and he hadn't had nearly enough sleep. So, Colleen was totally shocked when he came out of the room with a big grin on his face.

"I have something to show you."

She opened her mouth. "Tell me."

He shook his head. "No. It's a surprise, so you have to see."

"I've never been very big on surprises," she told him. Most of her experience with them had been bad. Her father's reckless decision to ride a bull when he had no experience of such things. His death. Her mother bringing home a new husband and son.

"It's not something bad," he promised. "Not a bug or a snake."

"I'm not afraid of bugs and snakes," she told him.

"Liar. At least about the snakes. I saw you when we were watching that nature show on television the other day. You were practically curling up in your chair when that diamondback came on the screen. You don't always have to be tough about everything, Colleen."

"Easy for you to say. They don't have snakes in Chicago. At least not the dangerous kind."

He lifted a brow. "Sure they do. Worse than diamondbacks, too, since they're the human kind. They're more devious."

She gave him a crooked smile. "All right, *show* me," she told him.

Dillon took her hand and led her to his computer. Then he sat down and keyed in a URL.

Within seconds a photo of a breathtaking house came on the screen. "It has everything all of you suggested would be necessary and then some," he said, giving her a virtual tour of the house.

"It's…a bit like a dream house," she said, staring at the big white stone building. "Like one of those places on cable television where the rich and famous live." It occurred to Colleen that Dillon actually might well be one of the rich and famous. At least in some circles.

"You could fit another small house inside each of the closets," Colleen said. "And all the windows and skylights make it seem so bright and inviting, but the yard and that huge porch are the best parts, I think."

"I'm glad you think so. I was thinking it would be a great place for a birthday party for Toby when that day comes."

"He'll be a star with all of your friends." Which only reminded Colleen of just how far apart their worlds were. Of course, Dillon would have lots of friends in Chicago. Women friends. Ones who were going to adore Toby and desire Dillon.

"So, you're buying it," she said, cutting off the sadness that was stealing over her. "That's so wonderful. You're on your way." Even though pain was rushing through her at the thought that he would, inevitably, be leaving soon.

He stared at her, long and hard. "Thank you," he

said. "My thanks to you and the other women, too. All of you knew what I needed when I didn't, and I'm grateful."

Over the course of the next few hours, everyone got a taste of just how grateful Dillon was. While he went on an errand and took Toby with him, a delivery truck arrived. Inside were flowers and seeds and bedding plants for Gretchen, a selection of the latest princess-style romance movies for Julie and a whole assortment of gourmet cookbooks for Millie's kitchen.

"That man remembered all the things we said when we were planning his house," Millie said. "Can you believe that?"

Gretchen turned her delighted eyes from the flowers to Colleen. "But what about Colleen?" she asked.

Colleen shrugged. She was so touched that Dillon had gone out of his way for her friends who had so little. And she was sure that Dillon was trying just as hard as she was to put some distance between them.

"I only told him to make the house safe. And he's already making *my* house safe," she reminded them.

It was true. Dillon had put in long hours. After the porch was finished, he had moved on to repair cracks in the walls, checked the electrical and heating systems and fixed what he felt were a few inadequacies. He'd made some changes at the bunkhouse and done some roof repairs on both buildings, driving himself relentlessly whenever he had the time.

"What more could a girl ask for?" she asked her friends.

"Good point," Julie said. "It's not every guy who'll climb up on a second-story roof for a woman. He must really like you."

"I...that wasn't what I meant at all," Colleen said, feeling her face grow warm.

"What did you mean?" A low, masculine voice sounded outside the open window and all the women jumped. Julie squealed.

"Were you eavesdropping on us?" Colleen demanded as Dillon came through the door.

"Absolutely," he said with a grin, catching her off guard.

Her eyes widened. "Aren't you the honest one?" she asked.

"Actually, I wasn't really eavesdropping," Dillon confessed. "Toby and I just got here. We were out on an important mission, weren't we, slugger?"

Toby stared up at his dad, his eyes wide. It was obvious that he was fascinated with Dillon. *And why not?* Colleen thought. *All the rest of us are fascinated.* She did her best not to ask what his mission had been. If he had wanted her to know, he would have said so.

"What mission?" Gretchen asked.

Colleen gave her employee and friend a "shush" look.

"I'm glad you asked," Dillon said. He pulled a bag from behind his back. "Because I really could use some feminine advice. There's this woman I want to take to dinner to show her my appreciation for all she's done for me, but I have it on good authority from Nate, the man who apparently runs the only department store within thirty miles, that there aren't any hot restaurants in town."

Millie snorted. "There are only two restaurants in town and only one of them has edible food."

"You must know Nate, too," Dillon teased.

"I have taste buds," Millie said with a laugh. "They work. If you want to go to dinner, go to Yvonne's."

"Thank you. I fully intend to, but since even Yvonne's doesn't appear to have the panache I was shooting for, I was afraid my gift would fall short."

Colleen wanted to tell him that she didn't need a gift, but since he hadn't said anything about the gift being for her, she couldn't very well do that.

"Fortunately, Nate and Yvonne and I made some special arrangements. Millie, do you think you can watch my little guy here for a few hours?"

Julie and Gretchen were already starting to whisper, loud enough to hear. *Special arrange-*

ments. What could those be? But Millie just smiled. "Yvonne is a good friend of mine," she said. "And of course I'll watch the baby. He and I are book buddies. We love reading stories. Besides, I want to make sure this special event takes place, too."

Now Colleen was getting flustered. "I don't like surprises," she reminded Dillon.

"I know. But this is a good surprise. I hope." Millie took Toby, and Dillon reached into the bag. Inside was an envelope, an ivory silk scarf and a bracelet. The bracelet consisted of gorgeous bits of garnet glass set in gold. A solitary golden heart was centered between the glass and golden chain.

"I asked Nate for the best piece of jewelry he had and he showed me this. I…at first it seemed wrong to give you something you had made yourself, but the longer I looked at it the more right it felt. You have so many of your works here, but only one piece of jewelry." He indicated the solitary bit of green glass on the black satin cord around her neck.

"I keep it to remember who I am and what I need to do and to forget," she said, fingering the delicate bracelet. "But this…it was my favorite, too. Too fragile to wear on a ranch. Nate paid me well for it."

"I hope you'll allow me to return it to you and accept the scarf. You'll have a place to wear the bracelet, since we won't be on the ranch tonight if you agree to accept my invitation."

He nodded toward the envelope and she opened it with clumsy fingers. "'Mr. Dillon Farraday requests the company of Ms. Colleen Applegate at table six at Yvonne's dining emporium at seven o'clock tonight. Dress is semiformal.'"

Colleen's skin felt suddenly tight. Her limbs felt heavy. This sounded too much like a date. But it wasn't a date. She knew that. "Just two friends having dinner, right?" she asked.

He smiled and tilted his head. "I hope you consider me a friend. You've done me a major favor. *Many* favors."

Gretchen's eyebrows rose and Colleen glared at her. "He's talking about Toby," she said.

"I'm talking about Toby," he agreed. "Colleen has mothered him and taught me. But she's also a pretty good kisser," he told Gretchen, who hooted.

"Hmm, telling my secrets?" Colleen asked, trying to keep from blushing. "I haven't said yes yet."

"Say yes," he said. "I want you to have a night on the town. Yvonne is making something amazing, I've been told."

"At her dining emporium, too," Millie added. "I'll have to ask her about that name. Usually she's just plain old Yvonne's or at best Yvonne's diner."

"Tonight's different," Dillon said. He waited.

"I can't disappoint Yvonne," Colleen said softly. "Besides, you've piqued my curiosity. I want to see the difference between a dining emporium and a diner."

"Oh, and there'll be entertainment, too," he promised. "I'll pick you up here in an hour, all right?" Then he winked at her and left the room.

"Entertainment? I wonder what that could be," Julie said. "Yvonne's never had entertainment before."

"I don't know, but I hope he kisses you again," Gretchen said. "He made you blush. I don't think I've ever seen anyone fluster you enough to make you blush. It looks as if it agrees with you."

CHAPTER TEN

DILLON felt like a kid going on his first date...
which was ridiculous. He'd dated many women
over the years. He might not be good at making
a success of emotional relationships, but he had
never had a problem getting things off the
ground. The only problem here was that with
Colleen there was no chance of even the begin-
nings of a relationship. He had to be careful and
keep his desire in check because he could hurt her
if this thing between them began to take flight.
So, that couldn't happen. He couldn't let himself
lose control.

And it wasn't just Colleen who was at risk,
either. Already he knew that he wasn't leaving
Bright Creek intact. He was going to miss Colleen
like crazy when this was over, from that bossy
brave way she had of crossing her arms and con-
fronting things that scared her to the way she threw
herself into kissing and then in the next minute told
him that they couldn't do it anymore.

Colleen was an original, but he had it on good authority that she had never been taken seriously as a woman in Bright Creek. She had always just been one of the guys.

Not tonight. It would be different tonight, and Dillon hoped she wouldn't be embarrassed or self-conscious.

He moved into the living room. And stopped. And just…looked.

She was wearing a red dress. He'd never seen her in a dress. And her hair waved around her shoulders. She looked…beautiful. Stunningly so in a way a more petite, less curvaceous woman couldn't. But really, Dillon thought, it had always been what came from inside that made Colleen truly beautiful. Who and what she was, was written in her eyes, in her smile, in the way she stood and moved. But tonight…

"I like that," he said, when what he wanted to say was "I like *you*." On another day he would have, but tonight this felt too personal. She had wanted things merely to be friendly. So did he. "I see you're still wearing your red cowgirl boots."

"I didn't have any dress shoes that fit and no one else wears the same size I do."

He smiled. "Looks good, though."

She laughed. "Nice save," she told him. "Julie complained that if I ever got married, I'd probably wear these under my wedding dress. They're not her favorites. To me, they look okay…sort of, but I wouldn't go further than that."

"That's because you're not a man looking at an attractive woman."

"That's because I'm honest. I just hope no one laughs when I walk into the restaurant. Maybe no one will recognize me with makeup and a dress on."

Oh, they would recognize her all right, and if there were any men there who had thought of her as one of the guys, they were going to be in for a shock, Dillon thought. He held out his hand. She placed her slender fingers in his. He allowed himself to enjoy her touch for just a minute while they moved outside to the car before he held the door open for her. "Better put the scarf on," he told her.

"Is that what that was for?" she asked. "I thought I was supposed to wear it around my neck or my shoulders or something."

"You could do that, too, but you'll need it for your hair right now."

She did as he asked, and by the time they pulled up in front of Yvonne's and got out of the car Colleen was nodding. "That was so amazing," she said, gesturing toward his car. "I thought you were kidding about the scarf. The way that thing moves so fast, the wind in my hair…it was incredible."

"Don't tell Harve you already rode in the Ferrari," Dillon teased her. "He'll turn green."

She laughed as she and Dillon walked the few steps to Yvonne's and Dillon opened the door. "Oh, my," Colleen said as they walked inside.

Oh, my was right. He'd stopped in this afternoon, and he had to admit that the woman had taken the money he'd given her and worked a small miracle in a few hours. There wasn't much that could be done about the booths, but Yvonne had covered every table in cloths the color of fine merlot. She'd put wine-colored shades on the wall light fixtures and left the overheads off altogether. White candles burned on every table, and soft music was playing in the background. A few people sat in the booths looking shell-shocked and confused.

Yvonne came out of the back as if on cue, holding menus that could only have been run off today. They didn't look anything like the ones Dillon had seen earlier. Yvonne herself had undergone a change from her customary pale blue uniform with white apron to a tasteful black dress and heels. "Mr. Farraday. Colleen," she said. "Please follow me. Your table is ready."

She led them to a table in a corner, the only table in the room, one that had obviously come from somewhere else. Dillon couldn't remember what had sat in this space this afternoon—a dessert display case, he thought—but this square table set with china and crystal and roses had definitely not been here.

"It's so beautiful, Yvonne," Colleen said, touching the woman's hand.

"You exceeded my expectations," Dillon agreed. "This is just what I had in mind."

"I may be small town, but I'm not small-minded," Yvonne said with a smile. "I know what a romantic dinner should be like."

For a second Colleen looked frantic and distressed, but Dillon touched her arm. "It's okay. I understand that you don't want there to be anything romantic between us," he said. "I'm not your type. But for tonight let me pretend," he said.

As he said it, he turned slightly, drawing Colleen with him. In a booth to their right, a group of men sat, staring. He recognized at least one of them from that day at the ranch when Colleen had blocked the exit. "Evening, men," he said. "I assume by the way you're looking at her that you all know Colleen."

At his words, they gave Colleen a once-over. And then they looked again.

"Whoa, Colleen, I…man, I just saw you at the ranch a week ago, but I wouldn't have recognized you tonight. You look…heck, you look hot. Hotter than Lisa Breckinridge. I mean Farraday," he said, nodding toward Dillon. "No disrespect to your ex-wife," he told Dillon.

Dillon shrugged. "I don't care about Lisa. Just so you know that Colleen is here with *me* tonight."

Colleen turned to the man. "But I'll still remember that you pushed me down in the mud once, Rob," she told him. "And you laughed at me and never said you were sorry."

The man's face turned red. "Well, I am sorry. I was young and stupid back then. And you…you were…"

"Felix Bamrow's ugly stepdaughter? That was what you called me."

"I know I did. I was sorry right afterward. You looked like you were going to cry."

"And then I kicked you in the shins, didn't I?"

"Yeah, you did. I deserved it, too. You want to kick me again? Or call me Harve Enson's ugly son? I'll stand still and let you."

Suddenly Colleen shook her head and gave the man a small smile. Dillon felt as if *he* had been kicked in the *stomach* the way she was looking at that guy. "I was never good at name calling and I don't kick men too much anymore."

"Do you let them apologize years after the fact?"

"Is it just because I'm wearing this dress? Would you have apologized if I'd been wearing my jeans?"

The man hesitated. "I don't know how to answer that. I don't exactly know, Colleen. You look pretty tonight but you still scare me when you're dressed for ranching. You always look as if you hate men, as if you'd welcome the chance to kick a guy or two."

"Maybe I haven't met too many guys who didn't deserve it."

The man nodded. "That's fair. I knew that your stepfather and stepbrother were jerks, and obviously, so were the rest of us." He motioned to the other men at the table, who hadn't said anything but were looking uncomfortable. Then he went back to his meal, but he didn't look too happy.

Dillon silently led Colleen to their table and pulled out her chair. After they were seated at right angles to each other, she leaned to the side and whispered in his ear, "Why did you do that?"

He shook his head, not knowing how to answer. "Do what?"

"Phrase things so that it sounded as if I was some woman you were pursuing. You did it so that those men would pay attention, didn't you?"

"Well, it makes me mad that, up until now, they haven't been able to see what's clear to me. Still, I probably should have consulted with you before I did that. You might not have approved."

"It could have ended pretty ugly," she said. "Rob or one of the others could have said something nasty."

"I didn't think any man could be so big an idiot that he would insult a gorgeous woman."

She frowned. "Rob Enson never thought I was gorgeous."

"That's because he's blind. The truth is that

you're gorgeous no matter what you're wearing. The fact that he doesn't see it when you're dressed for ranching just proves he's shortsighted, but believe me, Colleen, no one's so shortsighted and ignorant that they could miss your appeal dressed as you are tonight."

"But you didn't know that when you arranged this, did you?" she asked.

"I imagined what you would look like," he admitted, his voice deepening. Their voices were low so no one could hear, but his tone was such that a few heads turned when he made this comment. He knew he probably looked smitten. Frankly, he didn't care right now, because Colleen was looking at him with those clear, trusting eyes and she was smiling.

"Lisa was so stupid," she said. "While you were away, she must have forgotten how you say such pretty things. She always did need to hear those kinds of compliments."

And Colleen hadn't. She wasn't used to them.

"Colleen, I'm warning you, if you keep looking at me like that, I'm going to kiss you right here in front of the whole town."

"Well, that would be something else they haven't seen," she mused. "Me kissing someone."

Dillon growled.

Colleen reached out and touched his hand soothingly.

"Colleen, this is supposed to be *your* night. I wanted *you* to have the chance to be the queen for once. You get to shine tonight. You're not supposed to be worrying about my reaction."

"The queen? You darn silly man," she said, and when he looked at her, there were tears on her lashes. "You wanted me to have what Lisa had all these years."

"No, I wanted you to have more than Lisa had. Lisa is an illusion, an actress. You're the real deal. People need to see that. You deserve your due."

And then she laughed. Yvonne brought out the special meal she had prepared and Colleen turned to her. "Yvonne, this man is amazing. He did all of this to thank me just for babysitting that cute little baby of his. Isn't he something?"

Yvonne looked at Dillon. "I'm not arguing, Colleen. When he came in here today, I had to fan myself, he looks so good in jeans. Then I found out that he had this all planned for you. If I didn't like you so much we'd have to have a hair-pulling contest over him. As it is, I'm just glad it's you he's doing this for. You're the best. Enjoy the meal and the entertainment."

Colleen wondered what entertainment Yvonne was talking about. Wasn't having Rob Enson all but beg her to forgive him for his crimes entertainment enough?

Yeah, she was going to have to accept his apology before he left here tonight. It just wasn't in her to turn down a request from someone who seemed genuinely repentant. But she knew that none of that would ever have happened if not for Dillon.

She was more than entertained. She was enthralled. Too enthralled. Every time Dillon leaned over and whispered something to her, she wanted to turn so that their lips met. She wanted to wrap her arms around his neck. And it wasn't that he looked so amazingly handsome in his white shirt and black pants that did nothing to hide his tanned throat or the muscles in his thighs. It was Dillon himself, his very essence. The man was just dangerous. She was going to have to pull away or she would go up in a fireball now and be nothing but cinders when he left.

"There we go," Dillon was saying. "Those guys are good."

Colleen looked behind her to see that a trio of musicians had set up in the back of the restaurant. They were playing soft, slow tunes. Dreamy stuff.

"Dance with me," Dillon said and he drew her up with him.

"I don't know how." Suddenly, she was nervous. "I'll look like an idiot."

"I won't let that happen. I'll do all the work. You just shuffle along until you can follow my movements. I promise to keep it simple. And if all else fails, we can always resort to the standby slow dance. Just swaying together."

Oh no. Not that. That would be where she was held up against Dillon's chest, her arms draped around his neck and every cell in her body tight with desire. There was no way she could hide her reactions to Dillon from this crowd in that kind of a situation.

In the end, she didn't have to. Despite the wound that she knew still pained him, Dillon was a superb dancer and he led her through the steps with such ease that she didn't even feel as if she was learning.

In what seemed like mere seconds the dance had ended. She was staring up at Dillon and she knew that her eyes had to be glowing with naked desire.

"Mind if I cut in?" It was Rob, and Colleen blinked. For half a second Dillon looked irritated. No doubt because he remembered what had transpired between her and Rob earlier. He wouldn't let anyone crowd her if she didn't want it. She knew that. But Dillon couldn't afford to mix it up with anyone. The restaurant had filled by now as news of Yvonne's coup spread, and there were probably eyes and ears in this room looking and listening. There would be reports made to Lisa.

"All right, I forgive you, Rob," she said. "Since you seem sincere in your apology, and since you're

Harve's son and I like him. You just keep in mind that I'm not a very good dancer. No snickering or name calling."

"I don't do that stuff anymore," Rob said. "And I'm not such a good dancer myself."

Colleen tried to concentrate on the man she was dancing with. She didn't want anyone to notice that her gaze followed Dillon as he walked away, but it was almost impossible for her not to glance his way now and then as the dance progressed. To her dismay, she saw that Bill Winters, Lisa's spy, the man Dillon had told her not to worry about, had come into the restaurant. He was standing in front of Dillon, gesticulating wildly, his hands in tight fists.

"Rob, I…thank you for the dance," she said and stopped dancing.

"It ain't over yet, Colleen." Then he saw where she was looking. He uttered a curse and she knew that there would be no chance to keep this private. Already people were starting to gather round.

"It's just a little too suspicious that all this stuff started now after you came to town," Bill was saying, practically spitting out the words.

"Bill, pal, I don't know what you're talking about. Maybe you need to sit down. You really don't look so hot," Dillon answered.

"I don't want to sit down and I don't *feel* so hot. Why should I when there are pictures of me on the

Internet on my knees in front of Lisa begging her to notice me. I don't know where you got those pictures, but I never said those things. I never was in that pose. Those photos were altered, those dialogue balloons were added by somebody and I don't know anybody around here who would have any incentive to do that. Except Colleen."

Colleen did her best to look blasé. "Bill, you know I'm not that skilled with computers. How would I know how to do something like that?"

"And what incentive would she have, Bill? Colleen has no reason to cause you grief."

"You do."

Dillon shook his head. "We've barely exchanged two sentences until now. What would I have against you?"

Bill was looking around wildly now. He obviously couldn't admit that he'd spread tales to Lisa and that he'd spied on Dillon and Colleen when no one was supposed to know that. "I don't know, but nothing like this ever happened until you got here. I want it stopped and taken down."

"You'll have to talk to whoever put it up there," Dillon said. "You'll have to figure out who in town has something against you. That's rough, buddy. When something goes viral, it's next to impossible to stop it. Could take some time. Sorry, but I have to go now. My son gets up early in the morning and I have to be there for him."

"Hey, Dillon, how about showing us that car before you go?"

"Later, Harve. It's dark. You need light to do it justice."

Harve grumbled, but he didn't say more. Dillon smiled. He held out his arm and Colleen took it, falling into step with him. They didn't talk on the way home, but when they were finally in the house, had checked on Toby and were standing at the door that led to the back porch, Colleen looked up at Dillon.

"That stuff with Bill, was that part of the entertainment?"

"That was an extra I hadn't expected."

"Then you didn't put that stuff up on the Internet?"

He lifted a shoulder in dismissal. "I have friends and employees who live for all the quirky sites on the Internet. They know how to use a computer and how to send a message out so that it multiplies and hits its target. I might have indicated that a rumor might be helpful as long as it wasn't anything that would negatively impact Toby and me. Beyond that, no."

"It *was* pretty funny. Bill deserved that."

"I don't want him to think that he can threaten you. Now, he knows there are ways to get at him if he misbehaves."

"Thank you," she whispered.

"It's a little thing."

"Tonight wasn't a little thing. The restaurant and Yvonne and Rob and the music. I felt just like any other woman tonight."

Dillon groaned. "Colleen, you are never going to be just like any other woman. You are so much better."

"You make me better," she said, and then he was pulling her into his arms, his mouth covering hers and it was...so good, so right, so not nearly enough.

Suddenly, Dillon pulled away. "I better go before I do something that can't be called back."

Colleen looked at the door that she locked every night. "I put you out here because I didn't trust you at first, but..."

He stopped her with a fierce kiss. "Lock the door tonight, Colleen. Don't trust me, tonight or ever. This door is all that keeps me honest and away from you. You have to continue to be who you are after I'm gone and if I touch you...too much, I'm afraid it will show. People will know. It will change you somehow and make things more difficult for you. Lock the door."

She took a deep breath. She ignored the yearning in her heart and the pain of what could never be.

"I'll lock the door," she said. But as she put words to deeds, she knew that it was already too late. She'd let him into her heart and she already *had* been changed. The question was, who would she be when he and Toby were gone? What was she going to do?

CHAPTER ELEVEN

THE next morning, everything went south. Dillon was doing one last job, repairing a window that had been leaking during heavy rains when his telephone rang.

He answered it and listened. "Lisa's back in Chicago, Jace?" he said. "All right, I need you to find out what that's all about and what her plans are. Is she staying there? Just passing through? On her way here?"

But he didn't have to wait long for Jace's call. Within hours Lisa herself had checked in. "I'm home," she told him, "and I'm settling in. I'm nesting."

Dillon's blood temperature dropped ten degrees. "What does that mean?"

"Probably what it sounds like. I'm feeling very domestic. Very maternal."

"That's nice, Lisa. That's…fantastic. I'm wondering why you're telling me this."

"Why wouldn't I tell you? You're my ex-husband. We share a child. A child who's grown to be very cute and adorable, I understand." Then she hung up. Dillon swore.

Almost immediately, Colleen was there. She'd been inside with Toby, but now she came outside with him on her hip, which looked…right. He didn't want to even begin to tell her about the phone call. And yet he had to.

Quickly, he relayed Lisa's message. "She didn't ask for money," he said.

"She wouldn't. If she said it, then there would be a record of that, and if money is what she really wants, then she needs ammunition against you. She won't give you any to use against her."

"And if I just flat out offered her money on the chance that that's what she's after, she could use that against *me* in court by telling the judge I tried to bribe her."

They stood there looking at each other. Colleen's lips were nearly white, she was so obviously stressed. Dillon felt panic beginning to rip through him, and yet…he remembered his own childhood, wanting the attention of his mother and father. "If I thought there was a chance that she *really* wanted to be a mother to him…" Dillon began.

Colleen bit her lip, then nodded. "A child should get a chance to know both his parents."

"Yes. If I thought she cared about him even a

little, I'd make sure that she had the right to see him. But I'm not letting her take him from me, and if it's only money she's after, if she's trying to somehow use him…" Dillon's voice was hard.

Colleen reached out and touched his arm. "You can't let that happen."

"I'm not going to let it happen." There was no question that it was time to return to Chicago now, not next week. In addition to the problem with his business and his out-of-town project manager, he had territory on the home front and on the baby front to guard. He had to dig in and get ready in case Lisa made a move that would affect Toby.

"Let's go figure out how this is going to play out. What steps you have to take to stay ahead of her when you go back and how you can make this turn out right for Toby. I assume you've already spoken to your attorney."

"Of course. His advice is practical and sound. Don't make any wrong moves. Be a good father and a good person. Make friends. Make connections, especially in Chicago, since I've been away a while. It doesn't hurt to have good, strong character witnesses in the community."

"All right, then, you…you and Toby will go home tomorrow instead of next week. You'll furnish your house and you'll do all the things you've been doing and more." Her eyes were dark. Haunted, but she was standing straight and tall.

Not flinching, even though Dillon knew her heart was breaking over the loss of Toby.

Julie was walking past just then. "Dillon and Toby are really leaving, then? For good?"

Those last two words seemed to say it all. They spelled out the finality of this move. He was leaving *for good*. The stark truth of that thought caught Dillon off guard, and Colleen must have felt it, too. She put her chin up the way she did when she was trying to act as if she was unaffected by things that hurt.

Dillon understood completely, because inside he was howling. With rage. With pain. He hadn't been ready to break this off just yet. And not this way.

"But who'll help you set up that big house?" Julie asked. "More importantly, who'll watch Toby when you're at work or just not home? Won't your ex-wife…won't Lisa jump right on that if the person you hire scares Toby or isn't totally perfect? You need someone who's special, someone who Toby is going to love and who is going to love him right back, so you can't just go rushing in to hire any old person."

Dillon had been thinking the same thing. When he looked at Colleen, he knew she had already started to worry about those things, too.

"You really need more time to set the scene and set things up and find someone to help you with Toby," she said, "but…"

But he didn't have more time. What he needed was Colleen by his side for just a little while longer. What he needed was the impossible. He rubbed his hand along his jaw. He couldn't ask her. She had this ranch to run. She'd already given him too much, and besides, he knew that part of the reason he wanted her with him had nothing to do with his child. That wasn't fair to Colleen, not when both of them knew this thing between them wasn't going anywhere.

Colleen exchanged a look with Julie. Then she nodded, some feminine exchange that Dillon didn't understand.

"The others can manage alone here for a short while. If you need me, if you'll let me, I'll help you interview people and find the right person to be a nanny for Toby. I'll help you get your house set up and I'll help you show everyone just how dedicated to your child you really are. I can do this…if you…that is, if you want my help."

Dillon gave her an incredulous look. "I don't know which of the ignorant men in this town killed your confidence, but I'd like to kick every one of them over a cliff. If I want your help…Colleen, do I look like a crazy man? If you're offering, I'm accepting." Even if it was insane. Even if having her near and knowing she would only be in his home for a week was going to be a rough bit of knowledge to live with. A week was one week more than he had had just a minute ago.

"You two are going to have a lot of work to do," Julie continued. "Good thing that house is empty. You're going to have to close on it and furnish it in only days. There aren't even any beds in the place."

"There will be by the time we get there," Dillon said. "You all figure out everything you need to tend to before Colleen leaves. I'll tend to the Chicago end of things and then…Colleen?"

She looked at him.

"Before we leave I have something I have to take care of. In town. If you'd like to go with me and hustle up all the people I've made promises to, I would appreciate it."

Colleen looked confused at first, then she shook her head. "The car. Harve and the others. You don't have to do that, you know."

"Putting someone off until later is one thing, but a promise is a promise. I'm not going to say one thing and do another. Let Harve know that we'll be stopping by this afternoon on our way out of town."

"I will," she said, shaking her head, but Julie was already tugging her by the hand.

"Come on," Julie said. "We have to choose the right clothes for you to take to Chicago."

A look of distress came over Colleen. "Clothes? You know I'm awful at picking out clothes."

"I know. That's why it's lucky you have the rest

of us. We'll make sure you don't dress like a scarecrow...or a cowboy. Dillon needs to impress people."

For half a second, a look of terror came into Colleen's eyes before she managed to shutter it. His fearless Colleen, who had faced him down and stood off half a dozen men she thought were going to bother him and Toby, was afraid of embarrassing him by wearing the wrong clothes.

Just let one person in Chicago insult her, he thought, *and they'll have me to deal with.*

And wouldn't that be just great? If he stepped out of line at all...if he ended up in the newspapers or on a police blotter or even in the society gossip pages where he'd appeared before...when he got married...

Dillon felt like swearing, but that wasn't going to happen. He had to be on his best behavior. But he was going to protect Colleen, too. That was just nonnegotiable.

Tension filled Colleen's soul. She was flying blind here, heading into completely unknown territory and risking her heart in ways she couldn't even begin to imagine. She'd never even been outside Montana before, certainly never to a major city like Chicago. And to go there with a man like Dillon who, from the looks of his car, really was used to the best...

A vision of Lisa came to mind. The best,

everyone had always said. A woman who knew how to dress and wear makeup and get her way when she wanted to. And she always wanted to. She wanted something from Dillon, something that might hurt him and Toby.

Not going to happen if I can help it, Colleen thought. So there was no turning coward now. She put the last item in her suitcase and took a deep breath.

"I'm ready," she called to Dillon.

And the next thing she knew all her friends were hugging her.

"Don't get too fond of Chicago," Millie said, looking a little teary-eyed.

"But have fun," Julie said.

"And call," Gretchen added. "Take pictures so we can live vicariously."

Suddenly Colleen felt grounded. Especially since Dillon was watching them with such affection in his eyes. He had been so good to her friends, these women who needed the goodness that had been denied them in the past.

"I'll do my best," she told everyone. "But you know I'm not going to sightsee. I'll be there to help Dillon."

"Yes, but surely you'll see at least some of the city."

Dillon was laughing at Julie's impatient tone. "Don't worry," he told her. "If you think I'm going to keep her chained up in the nursery, well, I hope you know me better than that by now. I have a couple of social events where having an attractive woman on my arm will be a real asset, and of course we'll have to tour the city so Toby can see his new hometown."

Colleen rolled her eyes. "At his age, I doubt Toby's anxious to join the sightseeing set. And you can't take me to a social event. I won't fit in."

"Sure you will, and just in case you're worried about not having the right clothes, I already had my secretary buy you a couple of dresses and put them in the closet at the house."

"Dillon! You can't do that!"

"It's done. And don't deny me the pleasure. I can certainly afford it."

She shook her head. "We'd better get going before you tell me that you've bought me a castle."

"Colleen, why didn't you tell me that you wanted a castle?" he teased.

"I'm telling you now," she said in a teasing tone. "A gold one. With pink turrets and…and a unicorn." Her smile grew. "Hah! Just try to get your secretary to come up with one of those."

And with that, she took Toby from Millie and headed out to the car.

"You are going to be a handful," he said to her back. But he sounded pleased. For some reason that made her heart ache.

* * *

When Dillon pulled the Ferrari into a spot in front of Yvonne's, got out and took Toby out of his car seat, Colleen noted that the crowd of retired men in the chairs in front of Yvonne's was bigger than usual. In fact, this was a standing room only crowd. She walked around to the sidewalk and held out her hands for Toby. "I think you'll need both hands free. These men are going to want a show."

"And a ride," Harve said. "If that's possible."

Dillon smiled. "We can fit three at a time. Harve, why don't you drive us around the town, show everyone what this car can do, and I'll explain about the finer points of this vehicle."

"I hear it's made of aluminum," one man said. "That's one sweet little car. I wish my son was in town. He'd love to ride in this."

"Maybe if I'm ever out this way again," Dillon promised. But, of course, Dillon wouldn't be out this way again, Colleen thought. She'd known that all along, so why did her heart hurt?

Deal with it, she told herself and went into Yvonne's with Toby in tow.

For the next forty-five minutes, Dillon gave tours, let the men drive alone and at one point, drove out into the country so that one elderly man could give his grandson a chance to ride in the sleek car. "I couldn't deny a guy a chance to be a hero in his grandson's eyes," Dillon explained with a shrug.

"You're a softie," she said.

He shrugged. "Kids deserve to have a little un-expected excitement now and then."

And so do you, Colleen thought. But for the longest time all he had had was worry. The man had left the business of his heart, gone off to war, been injured and now faced the possibility that the woman who had betrayed him might try to harm him yet again.

If I can help him stop that, I will, Colleen thought. *But how do I stop myself from getting in deeper than I already am?*

CHAPTER TWELVE

IN THE end, Dillon had hired someone to drive the Ferrari home and a private plane to fly him, Colleen and Toby to Chicago. He just couldn't ask her to spend more time away from the ranch than she had to. They were both weary and wary enough already, and Toby was still young for a long, cross-country trip.

Even flying, by the time they stumbled into his house, it was late. Toby was asleep, and Dillon knew Colleen had to be tired, but…

"This is totally amazing, Dillon," she said, wide-eyed. "I don't know who you hired or how they worked so fast, but whoever he or she was, they knew what they were doing. This place is furnished so beautifully." She ran her hand over the honeyed wood of a table.

"And the forest-green and gold against all the hardwood floors makes everything look cozy and warm and inviting. And all those windows…the lights of the city are like a million fireflies. Toby will love it here when he gets old enough to notice the details. Or when he wakes up," she said, kissing Toby's soft baby curls. "I guess we'd better get him right to bed."

But no sooner had they located the nursery and gotten Toby off to sleep than Dillon's telephone started ringing.

He excused himself, took the call and immediately got another one. By the time the tenth phone call had come through, Dillon had had enough. He recorded a new message, begging off until the morning, telling all callers that he and his son were going to sleep and then he turned the ringer down on the phone.

"Looks as though your admiring public has found you," Colleen said softly. "You're home. Or maybe it was business and…I'm sorry, none of this is my affair."

"Jace thought it would be a good idea to broadcast the fact that I was returning to town with Toby, that I had a new house and was putting down deep roots. Most of the calls were old friends and acquaintances wishing me well."

"But not all?"

"One was work. And one was Lisa telling me that she would be over to see Toby first thing tomorrow."

The two of them stared at each other. "We'd better make sure we're on the same page, then," Colleen whispered. "I don't want to say the wrong thing and make a mistake that might cost you everything." She looked genuinely worried.

"You couldn't. Just be yourself and tell the truth. You're here to help me hire a nanny and get settled in with Toby, because Toby is used to you and you know what he likes."

Colleen bit her lip, but she nodded. She took on that serious, determined look that made him want to hold her and promise her that the world couldn't harm her anymore, that he wouldn't let that happen, even though he knew he wouldn't be around to fulfill that promise. "I *do* know what he likes. I *am* here to help you," she said. "Not trying to lie makes it easier. I'm not a good liar, although…"

He tilted his head as she hesitated.

"I would lie through my teeth if I thought it would help the two of you."

And just like that, every good intention he had about keeping his distance flew away on firefly wings. He framed his hands around her face and kissed her. Gently. Once. Twice. More times than he cared to count, because once he started kissing Colleen, his mind turned fuzzy and warm. He was dazed, confused, uncaring of anything except staying with her softness, keeping his mouth against her skin, holding her heat against his body. Giving in. Giving up. He wrapped himself around her, curled her body into his.

And all the time he was doing that, she was stretching forward, tugging him closer, kissing him back. Turning him into a mindless madman, a collection of desires and not an intelligent thought in his head.

"Kiss me again," she told him. "I love it when you kiss me."

He kissed her, and she moaned. She settled against him.

He slid his hand down her side, over her curves. Learning her. Memorizing her. Knowing that he had to memorize her, because soon memory would be all he had. This was…this was insane and he didn't engage in insane gestures. He didn't like things to slip out of his control. He didn't want to want what he could never have. He'd done that already. He'd regretted that too many times, and yet…

"Colleen," he whispered. "You're fire, you're magic. Touching you is like a dream and…"

He felt her shudder and then still beneath his hands. "You're right," she said. "This isn't real. It isn't right or logical or practical or…we both know that this…you and I have a purpose. That's what we both wanted, what we came together for. We're both nervous, fearful of what's going to happen in the next few days or weeks and that's why we're doing this. We have to stop."

Dillon stopped. She was wrong. He hoped she was wrong. He wasn't just using her to avoid facing the uncertainty of tomorrow. She wasn't just a crutch like the cane he had used when he first came to her house. And yet…what was she? She wasn't his, and she…

"You're probably feeling out of place. I know this is the first time you've even been out of Montana," he said. "I shouldn't have taken advantage of that out-of-kilter feeling. Come here. Come with me."

She was shaking a little and he wanted to soothe her, to warm her, but he was afraid of what would happen if he touched her again, so he simply wrapped a throw from the arm of the sofa around her shoulders. He led her to the computer that had been set up in a nearby room, sat her down and clicked on some keys. "Montana's an hour later than we are here," he said. "Everyone will still be awake."

Within seconds, Millie came on the screen and then the other women of the Applegate appeared. Colleen blinked. She turned to Dillon.

"Gretchen and I set it up before you left. They need you to be within reach, and I didn't want you to be homesick. Being able to see them makes it easier, I hope."

She blinked hard a couple of times. "You're making it very hard for me."

"In what way?" Dillon said.

"Before you came to the Applegate, I was happy believing that men were necessary to the world but not people I wanted to let into *my* world. Now, because of you, I've had to change my mind about men. Some of them are worth getting to know."

But as Dillon left the room and left Colleen to her conversation, he wondered why her words didn't make him happy. Of course, he knew the answer to that. Now that Colleen had opened her doors to men, she might meet one she would allow into her heart forever. Some good-looking cowboy might win her someday. He'd help her with her horses, he'd sleep with her in the bed Dillon had never even seen.

And you should be happy for her, he told himself as he tromped up the stairs to his own lonely room.

Instead, he wanted to go downstairs, talk Colleen into sharing his bed tonight and being the first man to tame her and win her. It was a selfish thought, he told himself.

But when the morning came, he hadn't slept it off. Her name was the first thing he thought of when he woke up.

Colleen woke up disoriented. The first thing she remembered was kissing Dillon and wanting him to never stop kissing her. She wanted him to make love with her, and that wasn't something she'd really wanted with any man before.

Which made it a very bad idea, because that meant that he was starting to mean far too much to her. And her time with him was limited.

Besides, today Lisa was coming. Perfect Lisa. Maybe perfect Lisa would want Dillon back. And had Colleen ever met a man who could say no to the woman?

She squinted her eyes closed, trying to block the thought, then got up, got dressed and went looking for Toby. He wasn't in his room.

Barefooted, she padded downstairs. Still no Toby and no Dillon.

"Look who I see." Dillon's deep voice rippled through her body. Toby's coo fanned across her heart. She let herself out onto the deck where the two of them were sitting in the early morning pale light. And stopped.

"Dillon…" she drawled.

"What?"

"Why did you do this? *When* did you do this?"

He didn't pretend not to know what she was talking about. "Hey, I love your sculptures," he said, turning toward the huge yard where several specimens of her work were prominently displayed. There was one in the shadow and dappled light beneath the large branches of a tree and two in full sun flanking a walkway that led to a gazebo. And at the entrance of the gazebo, multiple wind chimes waved and softly chimed in the slight breeze.

"Dillon, I can go months without a single order."

"That's because you don't promote yourself.

Your work is never seen. I guarantee people will see these. And they'll love them."

"Are you trying to help me without seeming as if you're helping me?" Of course he was.

"Are you accusing me of not knowing great art when I see it? This," he told his son, "is beautiful and unique, just like the woman who made it. And you and I are lucky we got in on the ground floor before everyone finds out about her and wants a piece of the action."

Toby gurgled.

"Yes, that's what I thought," Dillon said. "He thinks I made a great decision," Dillon told her.

She laughed and shook her head. "Well, far be it from me to demand that someone send back something of mine."

"As if they would. So…are you ready to see the town this afternoon?"

"We're sightseeing?"

"We're being seen. I have it on excellent authority that if we show up in the right places—the zoo, Lincoln Park, the butterfly haven at the nature museum—we'll run in to friends and acquaintances who will, of course, remember later that Toby was getting the best of attention. They might even mention to the local gossip columnist that a well-known businessman has returned to town after a long absence with his very happy, very well cared for child in tow."

She smiled. "Isn't that a bit manipulative?"

"Totally. Ask me if I care. This is my son we're talking about."

"Good point."

"I'll do whatever it takes."

"And so will I," she said decisively.

But when the doorbell rang several hours later, just as they had finally decided that Lisa wasn't coming, Colleen felt less certain of herself.

"Dillon!" Lisa said, rising on her toes and kissing Dillon on the cheek. "You're looking as delicious as ever." She swept past him into the room, all long dark hair, violet eyes and petite beauty.

"Hi, Colleen. Where's my baby?" As if Colleen had been hiding him in a cave somewhere for the past few months.

"Hello, Lisa," Colleen said, but she didn't answer the question. That was for Dillon to do.

"He's still napping," Dillon said.

"Well, wake him up. I can't wait to see him. You won't mind, will you? I'm sure he'll fall right back asleep."

Which wasn't true at all, and Dillon knew it. He'd grown to know a lot about babies during the past couple of weeks and about this baby in particular. Toby was fretful and cranky when he was pulled out of sleep early and it took him a while to adjust. In fact, Colleen could see that Dillon was ready to say no, and she wondered what Lisa would do with that denial. Tell people he hadn't allowed her to see their child?

"Dillon, you're angry with me and who could blame you? I was a failure at being a military wife, wasn't I? I was so lonely when you were gone and…what can I say? I panicked, I filed for divorce. But now I have this pretty baby, and I'm his mother."

No word at all about the fact that she had clearly cheated on Dillon and had abandoned her child in order to enjoy herself in Europe with a parade of men.

Still, Dillon didn't answer. "You're not going to let me see him, are you?" Lisa finally asked. She blinked those big violet eyes as if she were going to cry.

Colleen wanted to tell her to stop it, that Dillon wasn't like other men. He didn't fall for those tricks, but he *had* married her and—

"Lisa," Dillon said, "I don't know what you're doing, but let's at least not play games with each other."

Lisa froze. "What—I don't know what you're talking about."

He scowled. "You threw him away as if he meant nothing to you."

"That's not true! Colleen, tell him how it was."

Colleen wanted nothing more than to tell Lisa how it was, that Dillon was exactly right, that Lisa hadn't seemed to care at all, even though she knew she had to be careful here. Push Lisa into a corner and she would bring out the rusty knives and fight dirty. Still, Colleen had to ask one thing. "Why didn't you even give me any way to locate you? What if something had happened to Toby and I needed your help or at least your signature on medical forms? I can't even begin to understand that."

"Didn't you care anything at all about him?" Dillon demanded.

Lisa's pretty face crumpled. "Stop it! Please… my baby. I came here because…I just want to see my baby."

Dillon's expression was thunderous, but Colleen knew Lisa's methods well enough to know that this was when she was most dangerous, when she was being deprived of something. The truth was that if Dillon didn't do as Lisa said, she could claim that he had kept her from Toby.

So, even though it felt completely wrong on many levels, Colleen stepped forward. "We know you want to see Toby. Dillon's just waiting for him to wake up."

Dillon's frown deepened.

"But, of course, we know how difficult it is to wait in a case like this. You and Toby have been apart so long," Colleen continued, rushing on. "So, we won't wait any longer. I'll be right back." She closed her eyes, crossed her fingers, prayed a little as she moved into the nursery and gently picked up the sleeping baby. He was adorable, he was so sweet, and as usual, he had wet his diaper while he was sleeping. "I'm so sorry, sweetie," she whispered to Toby, "but I really need your help. You'll need to wait just a few minutes until I change you."

Toby woke up and began to blink his eyes and cry in that choking little way that babies do. Ordinarily, Colleen would have sang to him, rocked him. She fully intended to do that, she hated herself for not doing those comforting things for him, and yet—

She walked out of the room to face a fuming Dillon, and Lisa wearing a determined if pale expression. "Here he is," Colleen said, handing Toby to Lisa. She held her breath. Lisa was small, she was pretty and she smelled of expensive perfume. Maybe Toby would like all that. Maybe he'd be just like every other member of the male population. And...

Colleen could barely bear to move on to the next thought, but...if Lisa truly didn't mind this wet and crying baby and opened her heart to him, maybe Dillon would eventually have to let Lisa into Toby's circle. He'd said that he would allow it if Lisa truly wanted it. *Did* she really want Toby? *Had* she missed her baby at all? A part of Colleen knew that she should want Lisa to love Toby. For the baby's sake, she tried to be open-minded, even though in her heart of hearts, it hurt to even try. And she prayed that Dillon would not hate her for having handed his son over to Lisa.

Toby howled. Lisa held him at arm's length. "You're very pretty, aren't you?" she asked.

Those apparently weren't the words he needed to hear. Her tone was strained. If she'd only pull him in and hug him, rock him the way Dillon had on that first day…

"He's still tired," Dillon said angrily, and he started to move forward.

Colleen looked into his eyes. *Stop. Not yet,* she wanted to say.

Her expression must have told him something. He stopped.

"I probably shouldn't have been so…so insistent that you wake him from his nap," Lisa said. "But I was so eager to see him. I've missed him so much. We'll…he and I will get to know each other better when he's rested. I'll come back another day. I guarantee it. I so want to be a family with him." She said all of this to Dillon. She widened her eyes; she softened her voice. And all the time she was doing this, Toby had gotten louder and louder.

That could have been because Colleen was looking at him and standing just out of reach. Maybe. He sounded so pitiful. His tears were breaking Colleen's heart. *I'm so sorry, sweetheart,* she wanted to say. And she was.

The louder he got, the stiffer Lisa became. Whether she realized it or not, she was inching him farther away from her body.

"Mommy will be back when you're not so sleepy, bunnykins," she told Toby. And then without even looking at Colleen, she held him out. Colleen whisked him into the next room.

"Just a few more seconds," she whispered to Toby, listening as Lisa's voice continued to murmur something to Dillon. It wasn't until Colleen heard the sound of the door clicking shut that Colleen pulled Toby to her.

"I'm never doing that to you again," she promised, rocking him and cuddling him. "Waking you up from a sound sleep—not even giving you a chance to adjust or get a dry diaper. I would never want to hurt you."

She kissed him again, she swayed with him and murmured to him.

His tears began to stop and she quickly got him out of the wet diaper and into a dry one, then cuddled him close again. When she turned, Dillon was standing in the doorway, staring at her.

"I'm sorry," she said, "but I was afraid that with both of us questioning and criticizing her, she might do something drastic, so I had to make sure of her true feelings for Toby. After all, she's his *mother*. I know it was wrong to make her look bad to her baby."

Dillon was shaking his head. "Genetics doesn't make a person a parent. I know that all too well. My parents were totally ill-prepared to love a child."

"She might get better at it."

"I'm sure she could, if she wants to. In spite of the fact that I hated her coming in here and just assuming I would turn him over to her after she's ignored him for months, I'll make a place for her in his life if she really wants to try."

Colleen nodded. "That's only right. I probably should have warmed him up for her a bit."

He gave her a funny smile. "She didn't warm him up for you a bit when she thrust him into your life. Somehow I doubt you complained or ran out the door, saying that you'd be back later when he was behaving more pleasantly."

"That's because…"

I loved him from the start, she started to say, but that would just complicate things. Instead, Colleen merely shrugged.

Suddenly Toby laughed.

"Does that mean you're ready to go see the town?" Dillon asked.

And as always, Toby looked at his father as if totally entranced by his voice. As usual, he gurgled and cooed in response to the sound.

"All right, then, let's show Colleen what Chi-town's all about."

They dressed Toby and put him in his stroller and went out into the city. Dillon showed his son and Colleen the sights he had already mentioned, and she discovered that he had a genuine affection for the city that couldn't be faked.

"You love it here."

"It's busy and bustling. A city that works and lives and breathes, night and day. It's the heartland. Chicago was built and then burned to the ground, and its citizens put their heads down and built it again. People work hard here and they play hard. It has grit and beauty all rolled into one."

"And a lake," she added.

"A magnificent lake," he agreed. "I'll show you that tomorrow."

And he did. For the next few days, when Dillon wasn't consulting with his assistants on projects they had in the works, when he wasn't visiting job sites and getting back into the swing of the city, he took Colleen and Toby everywhere, or as much as he could in a city this size.

And Lisa didn't call.

But they both knew she would, eventually. Dillon began to hear rumors, delivered by friends, that Lisa was embracing the prospect of motherhood. She was buying baby clothes and toys.

Maybe she really did want to be Toby's mother.

Colleen fretted and worried and hoped that whatever Lisa wanted, her wishes wouldn't hurt

Toby and Dillon. She tried to hope that Lisa meant what she was saying, because that would be good for Toby.

Even though her heart felt heavy at the prospect, her heart couldn't matter. She wasn't the important person here.

Then, three days after they arrived, Dillon came to her. "I have a dinner tonight." He was staring directly into her eyes, looking apologetic.

"Don't worry. I'll be fine here with Toby," she told him.

"Colleen, I want you to come with me. I need you to."

"But Toby…"

He cleared his throat. "Taken care of. Millie is on her way here right now. Her plane lands in ten minutes. I have a limo picking her up. Toby will have a loving babysitter."

Colleen blinked. She didn't know what to say, to think. "You could have asked me."

"I know we discussed the reasons you might need to play dress-up back in Montana, but I also know that while the real scary stuff in life doesn't faze you, big social events make you tremble a little. I was afraid you'd make some silly excuse about how you wouldn't fit in with my business associates and friends at a formal party."

"Formal?"

"A bit."

Since she had been on the verge of trying to make an excuse about how she wouldn't fit in *before* she heard about the formal part, she was doubly nervous now.

"Dillon…"

"Colleen, all my friends want to meet you. They've been waiting. Begging me. They're almost as bad as Harve was about the Ferrari. They're dying to meet this paragon I've been talking about."

"Me? A paragon?"

"And an Amazon. And a woman who made my child feel loved the first few months of his life. Jace, my assistant, especially wants to meet you. He hopes you'll wear your red cowgirl boots."

"He did *not* say that."

"Cross my heart. And he's going to be terribly disappointed if you don't show up."

"I can't believe you called Millie and that she and the girls kept this a secret."

"We all know how you are. You would have found some way to wriggle out of it."

"Are you saying that I would back down from a challenge?"

Dillon grinned. "I would *never* say that. I know that you once kicked a man in the shins. You're one tough cowgirl."

"Yes," she said, "I am. And I would appreciate it if, in the future, you trust me enough to come to me and ask me if I want to do something before you go off and take control of things." Although she felt a little guilty at that comment. She still felt bad about panicking and taking over with Toby that day Lisa had showed up.

"Let's agree to discuss things first in the future," he told her.

She nodded. But, of course, there wasn't going to be a future. Surely the business with Lisa was going to come to a head soon. Either Lisa wanted Toby or she didn't. And if she did, there would have to be a showdown and some ground rules set. There might be attorneys and judges involved. But it would have to happen soon or Lisa's failure to act would put her out of the picture. Public opinion wouldn't favor her. She would do something soon.

But not tonight, Colleen told herself as she went to get ready. *Tonight I'm going to a dinner with Dillon. As his date.*

Which wasn't exactly what he had said.

But Colleen needed to dream a little, to pretend a little. Soon enough all pretending would be done. But tonight was hers.

CHAPTER THIRTEEN

COLLEEN received a video call a few minutes later. Harve Enson came on the screen. "Hi, Colleen, the girls hooked me up so I could talk to you. I just wanted to tell you that even though Millie's on her way to Chicago, you don't have a single thing to worry about. The women are expert ranchers, of course, but I hear they can't cook worth squat and with you gone, there's too much work for two, so if it's all right with you, me and some of the other people in town want to help out at the Applegate. All of us here in Bright Creek are aware of how much you've done for the girls and we know we've been insensitive, unfeeling snots in the past. We want to make up for all that. So, if it's all right with you, we'll make sure that the fishermen pay their fees, we'll get people to cook and we'll help out in any other ways the ladies need us to."

Colleen was sure that her mouth was hanging open. Insensitive, unfeeling snots?

"Harve, I don't quite understand. I certainly appreciate your offer, but…this apology is unnecessary and…I mean…why now? You've known about the girls living with me for years."

Harve cleared his throat. Was his face a little red? Did he look embarrassed?

"I know all that, but when we were out riding around in the car the other day, Dillon explained things to us. He told us *all* the details. It's one thing to know something and another thing to know all the little things that make a man see a situation in a…a realistic light. I knew you hired Julie and Gretchen at a crucial time in their lives, but I always had the feeling that you were bent on teaching them to hate men. We all knew what your daddy and stepdaddy were, so we didn't exactly blame you for seeming mad all the time, but your anger made it easy to dismiss you. Then Dillon cleared things up for us. He told us how you cared for that baby like your own and how you protected the girls and stood up to him to make sure he was a good father to Toby and…well, he reminded us that you had tried to protect him, too. That you weren't against men, just injustice. After that, it didn't feel right, knowing that we were part of the problem, the ones treating you like a man and going on about Lisa in front of your face and all. So…that's it, then. And you know I don't like feeling as if I owe someone something. I want to do my part."

Colleen blinked. Her throat felt too tight. She had spent years being "one of the guys" with Harve, and she couldn't really stop that now. At least not right away. It would embarrass him if she cried.

"Harve, I would be honored if you would help out."

She cleared her throat and turned to look at Dillon. He had taken care of Bill Winters for her; he had cleared things up with Harve and…who knew what other men had been in the car that day and who Harve had repeated this tale to?

Harve smiled and then laughed. "So the Applegate isn't no man's land anymore?"

She laughed, too. "Don't push it, Harve. The Applegate is still our sanctuary. But…thank you."

At that moment, the doorbell rang and she said goodbye to Harve and went to greet Millie as Dillon opened the door. Millie gave the room an appreciative glance.

"Very nice," she said. "Now, where's my baby? I'm going to spoil him silly while you two are out tonight."

Dillon laughed. "Okay, but tomorrow I've got all kinds of things set up for you," Dillon told her. "You've got choices. I made sure I had tickets and entrance passes to a bunch of things, since I wasn't sure what you'd want to see and do."

Millie smiled and patted his cheek. "You're a

good man," she said as he directed her toward Toby's room.

Colleen's eyes felt misty. If her throat closed up any tighter, she wouldn't be able to talk. Dillon…that man…he had known that Millie had never had this kind of treat before.

She turned to him to thank him, but he cut her off. "You'd better go get ready. My friends aren't quite sure that you're real. I've talked about you so much and so much time has passed that they're starting to think that I've made you up."

The funny thing was, Colleen thought later, as she stepped into the room where the dinner party was being held, that she was beginning to *feel* like a fictional character. The woman she'd seen in her mirror earlier wearing the off-the-shoulder cream-colored dress and the three-inch lacy heels looked nothing like the Montana cowgirl she had always been. It was difficult to know how to act.

But she was barely in the door when a man came up to her and introduced himself. "I'm Jace, Dillon's assistant, and you have to be Colleen, the woman who makes those wonderful sculptures."

Colleen blinked. "Did Dillon ask you to say that?"

He laughed. "No, he just showed me your Web site and I saw the ones in his yard when they were first installed. I've ordered one for my rooftop apartment."

"I…thank you," she said.

"And I really loved the red boots in the photo I saw. You left them at home?"

"Waiting for my next race," she said with a smile.

"My first cowgirl. I'm honored to have met you. You *are* an original," he said. Which was a much nicer way of saying she was odd or different than Colleen had ever heard.

In no time a crowd had gathered around Colleen.

"Dillon gets all the gorgeous women," one man complained, and for a second Colleen didn't realize that he was talking about her. "Do you allow guests at your ranch?"

"Hardly ever, Tom." Dillon's voice sounded from Colleen's right and he slipped his hand around her waist. Her heart picked up the pace.

"You must be the babysitter, right?" a bejeweled woman asked.

"That's far too anemic and limited a term for what Colleen does," Dillon said. "Colleen takes care of people, both babies and adults. She creates art, she runs a ranch and she's a barrel racing champion."

"Barrel racing? I'd love to see footage of that."

"So would I," Dillon admitted. "Don't you have any video of that?" he asked her.

"No, but Gretchen loves to take pictures and videos. The next race I'm in I'll have her tape it and send it to you," she told him.

Because she wouldn't be seeing him anymore. But she wouldn't think of that right now.

But the question about barrel racing had spurred other questions, and Colleen tried to explain what it was like to live on a ranch, how big the sky and land were, how small she was in comparison and yet how the feeling of being small was...right.

"You love it, don't you?" a woman asked.

"It's who I am and it's what I know."

"You're a fascinating woman," one man in his thirties told her. "A rancher, and yet you seem perfectly in your element in this high-rise apartment surrounded by city dwellers."

"Well, we're not completely rustic. There are plenty of cowboy poets in Montana, and some urban dwellers who have relocated from more cosmopolitan areas. And even though Montana's miles from here, the Internet brings a lot of the world into everyone's lives, doesn't it? I'm sure we must share a *few* things."

"A love of art, for one," someone suggested and another person went looking for their hostess's computer, calling everyone to come look at Colleen's Web site.

The whole time they'd been talking, Dillon had been by her side as if he was guarding her. The darn man was supposed to be having a good time with the people he hadn't had a chance to see in a long time, not watching over her. So, when the group moved away, she stood on her toes and whispered in his ear. "You don't have to babysit me, you know. Your friends seem nice."

"They like you. And all the men want your phone number."

She gave him an incredulous look. "I don't believe you."

"Believe me. See that man off to the right looking daggers at me?"

She looked. There *was* a man staring at them.

"He specifically asked me if he could ask you out."

"What did you tell him?"

"I told him that he wasn't good enough for you."

Colleen opened her eyes wide. "What's wrong with him?"

But Dillon was prevented from answering by the ringing of the doorbell. The hostess frowned. "I wasn't expecting anyone else."

When she went to answer the door, Lisa swept into the room. "Nancy!" she said, giving the woman a hug and a kiss. "It's so good to see you. I love that red dress. You always look so fantastic in red."

A visibly startled and embarrassed Nancy stuttered and stammered and finally thanked Lisa, who gave her a glowing smile.

"I know. I'm sorry to just drop in on you unannounced," Lisa said, "but I've been meaning to call on you ever since I got back in town and…"

She looked around. "Oh. Look at this. What a

dunce I am. You're having company. I'm sorry. I'm so, so sorry." A look of distress came over her face. "I hope you'll all forgive me for barging in like this. I didn't know. Nancy, don't worry, I'll come back another day. We'll talk."

"Lisa, don't be silly. Don't go," Nancy was saying, smoothing her palms over the red dress. "Come in. You know almost everyone here, anyway. I would have invited you, except I thought…maybe…"

She looked at Dillon.

"Oh, that," Lisa said. "Don't worry. Dillon and I still talk. We share a child. Our lives will always be entwined." As if to emphasize that, she moved over to Dillon and put her hand on his arm. Now he was flanked by both Colleen and Lisa.

Immediately, Colleen started to pull free. Dillon didn't let go.

"Lisa," he said, nodding his head. "Colleen and I were just going to discuss some details about the ranch with Jace. You'll excuse us?" It was a command, not a question, but Lisa seemed unfazed. She looked, Colleen thought, like a princess, dressed all in white with her dark hair perfectly coifed and just the right touch of red on her lips and nails. And when she walked, her gait in heels was much smoother than Colleen's had been.

"Colleen, you look so out of place here in the

city. I almost didn't recognize you without your old work jeans."

I almost didn't recognize you without your tiara, Colleen wanted to say. But she didn't. Making that kind of catty comment would only cost Dillon in the end.

Besides, the fact that she had instantly wanted to strike out and defend herself by criticizing Lisa stunned her for an instant. She had never been averse to defending *others*, and she would physically fight when taunted by a bully, but despite the fact that she'd known Lisa was a phony in many ways, Colleen had never confronted her in that way. At all. Instinctively, she'd known that Lisa possessed attributes she herself never would. A fight with Lisa wouldn't be a physical one, like kicking Rob in the shins, and it wouldn't be a fair one, either.

So, Colleen had always lain low and stayed clear of Lisa's territory. There had never been any reason for conflict between them because the two of them posed no threat to the other one. Had that happened, Lisa would have won. Colleen had no feminine wiles, no tools like the ones Lisa possessed, and her confidence in herself was limited to the narrow sphere of horses and ranching. She hadn't even seen her art as an accomplishment but as therapy. It was being sold only because Julie had claimed they needed space.

But Dillon had changed all that. He had given her a confidence in herself as a woman that she had lacked earlier. A sense that she could demand things for herself when she needed to.

So, what did she need?

She needed to know that Dillon and Toby were safe. Happy. Secure. Not being manipulated or used. But…how to accomplish that? Her usual, mulish methods of putting her head down and butting at the offender wouldn't work with someone like Lisa. If she did that, in the end, Dillon and Toby would pay the price. Especially given the fact that she was physically larger than Lisa, she'd look like a bully and Lisa would look like a fragile, wounded woman, a part she knew how to play well. Public opinion would, once again, be in Lisa's favor.

Colleen suddenly realized that everyone was staring at Lisa because of the "ranch jeans" comment she had made. And maybe because she still hadn't responded to Lisa's comment.

"Not that there's anything wrong with dirty ranch jeans, exactly," Lisa had dropped into the conversation somewhere while Colleen had been panicking.

"Except when there's a vulnerable little baby around who might be subject to all those germs," Lisa added when the room remained quiet, apparently stunned at her rude comment. "Do you realize how many horrible diseases ranch animals carry?" she added. "It's probably silly and ridiculous of me to worry, but…a mother worries about these seemingly insignificant things."

Now, some of the women and even some of the men were shifting their feet and murmuring. They clearly didn't want to insult Colleen but some of them had to be parents. Few of them would have any experience of ranching. Lisa's argument was beginning to sound sane, as if Colleen would unwittingly or uncaringly subject Toby to infection.

From the corner of her eye, Colleen could see that Dillon was nearing tornado stage. His brow was furrowed, his fists were clenched. He was going to wade into the fray and…and do what?

He's going to defend me. She knew that, just as she knew that anything he said here would be remembered, replayed in people's minds. Possibly used against him later. She held out her hand to stop him.

"I can assure you," he said, his voice steel, his eyes ice, "that Colleen would have moved heaven and earth to protect Toby. She subjected him to nothing that would have harmed him. And if you're implying that she did, then you never really knew her very well at all. Even though you dropped a newborn baby on her and walked away for months."

A collective gasp went through the group. Colleen felt her own heart pounding hard. Would this be all it took? The crowd would surely remember this fact. Not that it had been a secret, but…phrased this way in these circumstances, Lisa's abandonment of Toby seemed exceptionally bad and unfeeling. Would this be what helped Dillon to win?

"You're right. You're so right," Lisa said, her face crumpling, "but as a totally inexperienced mother…I was scared. I didn't know how to be a parent at all. I went to Europe. I took parenting classes. I worked on my confidence. Now, I'm…I'm ready to be a mother, finally." Her lip quivered. With her pale, pretty face she looked fragile, vulnerable, repentant.

Colleen could see that at least some of the people here forgave Lisa instantly with that speech. And what could anyone say to that?

Everyone was staring at Dillon, waiting for a response. Colleen wanted to help him, but anything she could say right now would be taken as interference by his friends, she was sure.

His jaw was taut, but he tilted his head as if digesting Lisa's words. "Every child should have a loving and attentive mother," he said quietly. "A woman who cares enough to go the extra mile."

Lisa smiled. She glowed. She practically smirked as she looked at Colleen.

"Of course, not every child gets that attentive mom. And Toby is used to the very best," Dillon said, looking at Colleen with that fierce blue gaze of his that did her in every time.

Colleen's throat practically closed up. She couldn't have spoken if she'd been able to think of anything to say. She wished she was alone with Dillon, but of course, that would have been rude to his friends.

So for the next hour, Colleen smiled and laughed and talked. She tried to pretend that Lisa wasn't in the room. She tried not to look at Dillon for fear that anyone watching would see the naked longing in her eyes. She'd learned early on in life that she couldn't have everything she wanted, and she couldn't have Dillon.

She didn't even know all that she said, who she talked to. Men, women, that man Dillon had warned her about. She feigned animation and a carefree attitude. And she must have done all right, because everyone smiled and laughed right back and no one seemed to be acting as if anything was wrong. They couldn't begin to imagine the rush of feelings that was going through her mind.

Lisa was going to challenge Dillon for the right to Toby. Somehow she was going to hurt him. Colleen couldn't let that happen. But she couldn't stop it.

So, despite the fact that Colleen liked Dillon's friends, the dinner seemed interminable. Finally, though, everyone rose from the table and Dillon moved to her side. "I'm afraid Colleen and I have to leave."

"It's still so early," their hostess said, but Dillon

shook his head. He took Colleen's hand and led her outside.

"We need to talk," he said.

CHAPTER FOURTEEN

THE house was quiet when they got home, but Dillon's mind was a whirlwind of activity. Colleen had been the princess of the evening tonight. Men had fawned over her; women had wanted to emulate her. She'd been beautiful and funny and witty and…Colleen, the woman he couldn't have. And Lisa had tried to insult her, hurt her.

Lisa was going to be a major problem. He was going to have to bring out the big guns. He hadn't wanted to go that route, but he would.

Later. Right now, he was consumed by the woman at his side. His beautiful, giving ranch woman, whom he couldn't hurt and couldn't have. When she'd spoken of her ranch tonight, it had been clearer than ever just how much she belonged there. And she'd been appalled about Nick, the man who had set his sights on her. Letting Harve help with the ranch while she had no option was one thing. Letting a man into her heart was another. And it was a sure thing that if she ever did go that route, it would be with someone linked to the land. Like Rob, Harve's son and a man who'd grown up with ranching, not a Chicago businessman.

But Dillon had been watching Colleen all night, breathing her in all night. When Lisa had insulted her, he'd wanted to insult Lisa right back, and it wasn't his way to beat up on a woman. When Nick had drooled over her, he'd wanted to warn the man away.

He was in over his head. He was falling for another woman he couldn't keep and he was going to lose her any day now. Already Jace had given them a list of nannies to interview. And Jace had great instincts. It wouldn't take long to settle on one. She was going to ride right out of his world.

"Everyone's asleep," Colleen whispered quietly, but the sound went right through Dillon's body.

"We're not," he said.

She gave a low, sexy laugh. "Don't try to be cute, Farraday. You knew what I meant. We were out partying, so we're excused for still being awake."

"You were a big hit," he said. "A Montana marvel."

"Your friends were being very nice."

He didn't answer right away. When he did he couldn't keep the anger from his voice. "I'm sorry Lisa tried to insult you. You shouldn't have been subjected to that when her battle is clearly with me."

She shook her head and the silk of her hair brushed the underside of his jaw. He breathed in the scent of her shampoo. "I can handle a little insult from Lisa."

"I don't want you to have to. I'm not letting her get away with it again."

She looked up, the dim light from the moon outside casting part of her face in shadow, part in milky light. "You can't battle her, Dillon. She knows how to get her way. I saw how it was the day she came here and again tonight. She plants doubts in people's minds and wins them over. She uses half-truths that are difficult to disprove. I've seen it."

He had, too, but he'd had Jace and the rest of his crew on the job. Lisa wouldn't get her way this time. And he didn't want Colleen taking a hit for him.

"I'm not letting it happen again," he said firmly. "You're not a pincushion or someone's punching bag."

"I'm not fragile," she argued, clearly a bit miffed.

Now it was his turn to smile. "No, not fragile but…Colleen, when this is over I don't want you to have regrets."

He pulled her against him.

"If you mean you don't want me to miss the two of you, it's too late for that. I will." She raised her arms. Her fingers brushed across his jaw.

He groaned. And then he pulled her closer. He kissed her deeply. "You make me do things I know I shouldn't do. I don't want to hurt you."

As if he'd pushed some sort of button he'd been unaware of, she pulled closer. "Only I decide who can hurt me. You can't hurt me. Touch me."

He snaked his arm around her and pulled her up against him. She was part of him, and he drank from her lips. He breathed in her scent. He wanted more.

"Colleen?"

"Your room," she whispered.

Together they somehow made their way up the stairs to the back of his house, where his room took up half the second floor. The door closed behind them. Colleen stepped forward, grabbed the lapels of his jacket and jerked down the sleeves. "I've been wanting to do that all night," she said.

He slid the strap of her dress down and kissed her bare shoulder. "Not as much as I've been wanting to do this."

"That's what you think." She pushed him down on the bed. He let her. Then he reached out and she slid right into his arms, right up against his heart. She lay on top of him and they tangled themselves around each other. He kissed her long and deep, again and again.

"You're very good at this, aren't you?" she asked, just before she kissed him back.

He laughed against her lips.

"What?" she demanded.

"It's a strange question to ask a man, to comment on his own prowess as a lover."

"Well, I don't really know what a woman is supposed to ask, since I've never actually done this before."

Dillon stopped laughing. He stopped kissing her. His heart was still slamming around in his body. He still wanted her as much as ever, but his mind was issuing warnings left and right.

"Colleen, you've never done this before and this…us, here, together…how much wine did you have tonight?"

She lifted her head and stared into his eyes. "I didn't have more than a sip and this…us…it's not the wine talking. Are you saying that you don't want to do this with me?"

The doubt in her voice broke him. "Colleen, I've been dying to do this with you for weeks."

"Then…"

"You've never done this."

"Are you afraid I won't be any good at it?"

He groaned and rested his forehead against hers, cursing himself.

"Because *I'm* a little afraid that I'll suck at it," she told him. "If I'd had some practice I'm sure I'd be better." As she was talking, still lying against him, every word echoed from her body to his, driving his temperature higher. The slightest movement she made brought her flesh sliding against his skin.

He couldn't stop himself. He kissed her hard, fiercely, possessively. "I don't need you to be better at it. You're already driving me crazy. But, Colleen, if this is your first, if this is your only… For now, anyway, I have to make it good for you. If it's not, if *I'm* not, it's all on me, not you. You understand?"

"Yes. I understand that you're trying to do one of those male domination things. Taking all the blame. But you know that's not my way. I'm a full participant. I just wanted you to know that I might be awkward and clueless and—"

"Don't say another word, Colleen," Dillon said, pulling her against him. Jace was right. Colleen was unique. What other woman would apologize in advance for being clueless when she was so clearly burning him up? His lips captured hers. He rolled with her so that she was beneath him now. "I'm going to tell you what I'm doing," he told her as he began to peel her dress away. "Just in case you're worried about being clueless. Right now I'm revealing all the parts of you that I've been dying to see for so long."

He kissed his way down her body as he drew her dress away from her.

"And I'm kissing all the parts of you that I've

been wanting to kiss," he told her as his lips brushed her curves, her soft skin, as her breath—and his—came quicker.

"And I'm—"

"Ripping your shirt off. Undressing you, too," she said, awkwardly but forcefully doing exactly as she said. Why had he ever thought that Colleen would be a recipient and not a participant?

"I'm kissing you the way I've been wanting to for a long time," she said, wrapping herself around him so that his breath hung in his throat.

He groaned, tangled his fingers in her hair and held her still as he kissed her, as he ran one hand down her body.

Their bodies tangled, they traded kisses. The fire grew hotter. Their whispers grew more feverish.

"Dillon, what—what are you doing now?" she asked.

"Driving myself crazy. Touching you…everywhere."

"Do that," she said. "Yes. Tonight. Just…tonight…do that with me."

Which only made this more pressing, more poignant, because yes, tonight would be their only night.

He placed his hands on hers, palm to palm. He kissed her lips, her throat. Lower, then lower still and then he rose up. "Are you ready? Are you sure, Colleen?"

Her answer was to meet him, to join with him. Together they tumbled through dark and light, thunder and lightning, sunrise and sunset, falling, falling, all control gone as they fell into bliss.

Dillon whispered her name hoarsely, collapsing and rolling with her, keeping her by his side.

But in the morning, she wasn't there.

Tonight, he remembered her saying. *I love her,* he thought, but he had agreed to her terms. One time, one night. Their days together were ending. He wanted to hold on, but that wasn't what she wanted.

Just one night. He had to free her in such a way that she could be happy, even without Toby. If there was a way, he would find it.

Colleen was a mess. A total mess. What had led her to sleep with Dillon when she'd already known that she was falling in love with him? Now, after a night in his arms, after an experience that still had the power to make her breath stop with wonder just thinking about it, she was lost. Completely and utterly lost.

I'm fine, she tried to tell herself over and over again, but the truth was that she was anything but fine. How was she going to survive this need to be with him, this desire to just hear his voice or see his smile or…more? What was she going to do? What if he discovered that she loved him?

Then she would be pathetic. He knew he'd been her first, her only, and he'd been concerned. Probably about this. That she'd make too much of it, get in too deep. He'd hated hearing Lisa try to insult her—how much more would he beat up on himself if he suspected that he was about to break her heart?

I'm not letting that happen, she told herself. Firmly. She had made a point of never letting others suffer when she could stop it. She had always been a woman of action, and action was called for now. She had come here to help Dillon set up his house, find a great nanny and make sure that Lisa didn't try to abuse her title as mother to manipulate and blackmail Dillon the way she had manipulated others in the past.

"Well, let's do those things," Colleen whispered. She was capable. She could do all of them, except…Lisa had never lost. At least as far as Colleen knew of. What to do? How to manage? If she just concentrated on this, she couldn't allow her hurting heart to sideline her.

She thought of all she knew about Lisa. About the "mother lessons" Lisa had mentioned the night before and about how Dillon had not had a relationship with his parents and would want Toby to know his mother if Lisa was genuinely interested in her child.

Maybe this *would* work out for Dillon and Toby. Maybe Lisa *was* changing. If that was so, they might all become a family, which would be good for Dillon and Toby.

But how could anyone read a person who had always made herself unreadable, a woman like Lisa who had been born playing whatever part was expedient?

Maybe you gave that person an audition, Colleen reasoned. There might be a way to find out some small bits of information…but she would need help, planning and a lot of luck. Colleen took a deep breath and went in search of the one person she knew would help her give Dillon the gift of truth. She tried not to think about what she planned to do next. Instead, she just plunged in.

When Dillon woke up and made his appearance an hour later, Colleen was in her bathrobe. "I'm sorry. I'm not feeling myself," Colleen said, trying not to look directly at Dillon.

His look of concern drove an arrow right through her heart. She knew he had to be thinking that she was experiencing buyer's remorse and regretting that she had slept with him, but what could she say?

"You won't mind showing me a bit of the town, will you?" Millie asked. "I promised Gretchen and Julie I'd buy some souvenirs and give them a report."

"Jace—" Dillon began, but Colleen drove herself to give him a wounded look, to appear appalled that he would send a substitute. Guilt trickled through her.

"I'd be delighted," he said, even though he looked worried. Colleen's heart was breaking just looking at him, but she tried to tell herself that this was necessary. As soon as they were out the door, she threw off her robe, revealing that she was fully dressed.

Forgive me, she silently told Dillon. *I have to do this. I have to at least try to help.* She had invited Lisa over, and the woman would be here soon. She hoped against hope that she was doing the right thing, because if she wasn't…if she was wrong…Colleen's stomach began to churn. If she handled this wrong, the fallout would be unthinkable.

So, by the time the doorbell rang a short time later, Colleen's heart was in her throat. She had to coach herself to go slowly, to make Lisa wait a normal amount of time. She had to pretend that everything was normal. As if anything could be, given this whole horrid situation.

Colleen only knew that the truth was important. To Dillon and to Toby. They deserved truth, love, everything. Not being blackmailed or threatened. So, if there was any way to cut through this game Lisa was playing, if there was any warmth in Lisa's heart at all, Colleen had to find it. And if there was no warmth or love within the woman…

She'll have to go through me to hurt the people I love. That was Colleen's last thought before she went to the door.

"Lisa, I'm glad you agreed to come by. Come on in the kitchen. It's sunniest there."

Lisa looked around as if expecting to see Dillon.

"I'm sorry. He's not here," Colleen told her. "I wanted to talk to you alone about last night."

"No hard feelings, I assume, Colleen? If you're referring to the ranch clothes line, I was just being friendly."

Colleen shook her head. "I meant the mother lessons. It must have been hard for you without Toby and now you're still separated from him, so today while it's just you and me, I thought you could have some quiet time to get to know him."

Lisa blinked. "I…yes. That would be great."

"I'll go get him out of his bed."

Lisa's eyes widened. "He won't be screaming like last time, will he?"

"No, he's been awake for a while." Colleen left the room and returned with Toby. "Sit right there. It's a good chair with enough room for you and the baby." She handed Toby over to Lisa as soon as the woman sat down. Then she prepared a bottle and handed it to Lisa, who was awkwardly holding the baby. Toby was listing slightly to one side.

"He'll be hungry," Colleen assured her.

"Hungry. Yes." Lisa poked the bottle at Toby. Fortunately for her, he knew what the bottle was about and latched on to it, drinking it quickly. When he had finished, Lisa looked up, triumphant.

Maybe the woman really did want to be a mother, Colleen thought, even though she was holding Toby away from her body as if he might explode at any minute. For Toby's sake, she hoped that was true.

"You'll probably want to burp him now," Colleen said. "I usually do."

"Of course. I know what I'm doing," Lisa said. She started to bring her hand back.

Colleen's eyes widened. "Softly!" she said, just in time.

Lisa's hand slowed. She began an ineffectual series of movements, barely making contact. "Takes a long time, doesn't it?" she asked, gritting her teeth. "What's that smell?"

"Baby," Colleen offered. "Most people like it."

"Yes. Very nice." Lisa smiled.

Just then, Toby did what he did so well. He spit up all over Lisa's hand, the curdled mess dropping onto her black dress.

"Uck! My dress!" Lisa yelled. "Here! Here! Take him. Give me a wet cloth! This is a Versace. Colleen, help me."

Colleen frowned, but she took Toby and cuddled him to her. She gave Lisa a damp cloth and watched as Lisa rubbed at the milk stain.

"In the future, you'll probably want to wear something less fragile when you're with Toby. These things happen."

Lisa frowned. There was a damp spot on her dress.

"Here, take this," Colleen told her, handing her an apron.

"Excuse me?"

"To protect your dress. Now that he's spit up all over himself, he needs a bath. Here, we keep the tub on the counter. Just…prepare the water and we'll get him all clean."

"Maybe you should prepare the water."

Good idea. Lisa might make it too hot or too cold. "All right. You hold Toby."

Lisa let out a long sigh. "*I'll* do the water."

Colleen let her, but she nudged Lisa aside and adjusted the temperature before she would let her fill the tub. "You must have forgotten about making sure it's not too hot," she said.

"Yeah, I forgot," Lisa said. But she took Toby when the water was ready and made a rather ineffectual attempt to clean him, holding him at arm's length. When she was done, Colleen handed her a diaper and gave her a pad to lay Toby on to change him. Lisa studied the diaper as if it were a puzzle. She started to put it under Toby. Colleen turned it around so that the diaper wouldn't be backward.

"I knew that," Lisa said. She tried to put the diaper on without touching Toby and managed to get it fastened, albeit with gaps at his legs.

Toby was getting impatient and starting to kick his legs around. He was starting to whimper. Up until now he had been relatively calm, willing to put up with the lady who had given him a bottle, but now his diaper was crooked and probably uncomfortable. He had managed not to gift his mother with the ultimate insult, but Lisa had barely gotten his diaper on and sat down with Toby when Colleen noticed that his diaper was already wet.

"At least he waited until he was wearing a diaper," she pointed out, but Lisa was holding him even farther away from her body than she had been before.

"You change him," she told Colleen. "I'll have a nurse to do all this stuff, anyway."

To Colleen's chagrin, Lisa looked as if she might cry. "Lisa," she said gently, as she took the baby, quickly changed him and turned to face the other woman. "*Why* are you doing this? You obviously don't really want to…to…" Be a mom, she had started to say, but that almost seemed too cruel. Even though she had no doubt that Lisa wouldn't have hesitated to say the same thing to *her*.

"I'm a year older than you. A year closer to thirty," Lisa said. "I don't even know who my father was, but my mother…we had no money. All those dresses I wore came from a thrift store fifty miles away. And I promised myself that I would have nice things when I grew up. But Dillon was so into his work that he didn't even look when I bought a nice purse or nice shoes. And he didn't care about parties. He was so boring, so into working and going off to save the world and…and boring. Still, when I divorced him, my unlimited supply of funds was limited. I need nice things, Colleen. I don't want to be my mother."

Despite the petulant, spoiled sound of all that, there was something so sad about it. "Nice clothes won't bring back the father you never knew, Lisa. You know that. They won't buy you the attention you want."

"I get plenty of attention."

"And just look at this baby, Lisa. You helped make him. He's wonderful."

Lisa looked at Toby. "He *is* pretty," she said.

"He's very pretty," Colleen agreed. "And he deserves to have…everything a child wants and needs."

Lisa froze. She looked at Colleen with cool, beautiful eyes. "And you think I can't give him that, don't you?"

Suddenly, Colleen began to wonder at her own audacity in testing Lisa to see if she had a trace of loving mother buried inside. She had lied to Dillon to set this up, she had taken control from his hands and now…

"I don't know if you can, Lisa. You don't really seem as if you want to take on the role of mother. And if this is just about money…if that's all you're after…"

"Then what would you do, Colleen? You know me. I go after what I want and I get it."

"Not this time."

Lisa smiled sadly. "He *is* a pretty baby, but I told you, I need things, and Dillon has money."

"Toby and Dillon aren't just tickets to pretty dresses."

Lisa shook her head. "I'm sorry, Colleen. I really am sorry it's come to this between you and me, because this is a contest you're going to lose. I never had anything against you when we were growing up."

"Maybe not, but you hurt people I liked. I'm not letting it happen again."

"So…all that stuff…the bath and the bottle was just a test to trip me up?"

"I'd hoped you'd pass it."

"And I hope you know better than to cross me." Lisa's expression was cold. Her pretty eyes weren't very pretty.

Colleen felt a trickle of fear slip in, but she refused to give in to it. "I know better than to cross you. I've seen how you fight, but I'll still stop you." Colleen heard the door open, but she didn't drop her gaze from Lisa. "I'll do whatever it takes. You're not going to ruin their lives for money."

"Of course I'll win, Colleen. I have all the cards," Lisa said, even though her voice sounded less certain than before.

Slowly, Colleen shook her head. She stared straight into Lisa's eyes. "You have powerful weapons, Lisa. They've helped you cheat and win for most of your life, but not this time. I have something better."

Lisa frowned as Dillon and Millie and Jace came through the door. "What do you have?" she demanded.

Colleen was extremely aware of Dillon's presence, but she couldn't allow herself to be distracted. "I have friends in Bright Creek. So does Dillon. And I also have a good memory. I know everyone you hurt. If I have to, I'll get down on my knees and beg them to tell their stories before a judge. I don't want to hurt you, but I'll do everything I can to keep you from harming Dillon and Toby. I promise you that."

"You'll lose."

For half a second, Colleen felt paralyzed remembering who she was and who Lisa was. Lisa had always been the best, the prize, the winner. Then, Colleen hazarded a glance at Dillon, who was studying her closely. But he wasn't interfering. He was trusting her. She couldn't fail him now. She raised her chin. "I might fail, but I don't think so."

"Why not?"

"Because you have so much more to gain by not fighting and lying. If this goes to court, at least some people will see the less attractive side of you. I'll force you to fight, and that won't be pretty."

"It won't be pretty for you, either."

"But that's why I'll win. Not being thought of as pretty doesn't scare me a bit. I don't need it."

Lisa paled just a bit. She tilted her head. "I never saw this side of you, Colleen."

"You never pushed me before."

"This…you said I had a lot to gain by…I assume by letting Dillon have Toby. What would I win?"

Colleen felt Dillon's eyes on her. She turned to look at him. His expression was indecipherable, but he hadn't taken his eyes off of her. She sensed the tension in him and she knew he wanted to take over, but he was still letting her have her say.

"Toby *is* a pretty baby," Colleen reminded Lisa. "And Dillon is a good and loving father who'll be fair in all ways. And if you don't drag Toby through the mud, you'll get to keep your untarnished image as the queen of the Lupine Festival. I won't try to make you look ugly in the eyes of the citizens of Bright Creek."

Lisa shook her head. She frowned.

"Don't underestimate her, Lisa," Dillon said. "You chose well when you chose her to care for Toby."

"I know that. At least give me credit for knowing that," Lisa said.

"I do," he told her.

"And just for the record," Lisa said, "I know there's been speculation about whether or not you're really Toby's father. You are. I was faithful until weeks after you went to war. He's yours."

"He was always mine," Dillon said, "but thank you for saying that."

And suddenly Colleen felt like an intruder. Her part here was over. Had she helped or harmed the situation? Dillon had complimented her, but would he, ultimately, end up regretting this day?

Colleen turned to face him. Her skin felt tight, her spirits low. Maybe she'd just made a mess of everything. "I'll just let you and Lisa talk now. I'm sorry that I lied to you about feeling sick. And that I didn't tell you I was going to do this when I know we agreed to be up front about our plans."

He still hadn't spoken, so she faced Lisa again. "What's between you and Dillon and Toby is between the three of you, but he's a wonderful little boy. You'll miss a lot by underestimating the joy of being with him."

Lisa shook her head. "Not everyone can be a mother, Colleen."

As Colleen knew all too well. "Maybe not. I happen to believe that people can change their lives…if they want to. I believe in leaving doors open."

Lisa studied her for long seconds. "I never really

knew you at all. You're more interesting than I thought. And maybe a little more dangerous. I could almost like you if I wasn't starting to hate you." But her voice held no antipathy.

Colleen shrugged. She started to leave.

"Colleen." Dillon's voice stopped her. "We have to talk."

"I know. When you and Lisa are done, I'll be upstairs."

She went upstairs and took out her suitcase and piled things in it. Millie had never unpacked. "I promise you," she told Millie, "that someday I'll make sure you get a trip where you get to see more, but...I can't stay here now."

Millie slowly nodded. "You love him?"

"I have to go home."

"But—"

"I really have to leave," she told Millie, zipping her bag shut. The shadow in the doorway told her that Dillon was here.

"Toby's in his bed, Millie," he said.

Millie didn't even ask what he meant. She just left the room.

Dillon stared at the suitcase. "You're leaving."

"I don't have any reason to stay any longer. I've talked to Jace and told him that I'm not sending his sculpture until he helps you choose the very best, most caring nanny in the world." Her throat was closing up. Getting the words out was so difficult.

"You did all that downstairs for me and Toby."

"I had to be sure she really didn't want him and that she knew it wouldn't be as easy as it's always been for her before."

"You didn't need to do this. Jace and my other employees and I had enough information about her actions in Europe to keep her from being able to threaten to take him from me. She's giving up. We reached a compromise."

Somewhere Colleen found a small smile. "Good. I'm glad. but this way…I'm hoping that she can claim that giving him up was her own choice. Even if I threatened her, I hope she knows I'll let her keep all the gold stars if she does the right thing. And maybe if the door stays open, she'll find a part of her heart for him. She's…I think she's still avoiding issues left over from her childhood, and I just didn't want her to be able to blackmail you. I had hoped that there was something maternal buried deep inside her. There isn't…yet, but maybe someday there will be."

He ran his palm over her jaw. "I know what this must have cost you. You're not a person who goes looking for trouble or controversy. And you've told me that you never mixed it up with Lisa the way other people did. To pit yourself against her…I…"

He kissed her. It seared her soul. She fought tears.

"I needed to do it," she said, "and look. Everything is great now. You and Toby have a wonderful house and a wonderful life and I've got to get home and start working on my sculptures again and make sure Harve hasn't run my ranch into the ground. It's been…it's been nice. It's been a pleasure getting to know you, Dillon."

How was she maintaining that calm, friendly atmosphere? Colleen had no idea.

"You could stay longer."

She shook her head. "No, I don't…I just… can't." She rose on her toes slightly and kissed him, then turned toward the door.

"I'll drive you to the airport."

"No, that's okay. We'll take a cab."

"Dammit, Colleen, at least let me get you home. At least let me send you in a limo and in my airplane."

And because she was wild now just to be away before she broke down, she said yes. Somehow she would keep from doing anything that his employees could report back to him.

She surged from the room. Millie was waiting with Toby in her arms. Colleen took Toby from her and kissed him.

Darn those tears. She looked through them at Dillon as she handed over the little boy.

Love him, she wanted to say, but she knew he would. Love *me,* she wanted to say, but she knew he couldn't.

"Goodbye, Dillon," she whispered. "Thank you for sharing your child for a while." Then she stumbled out of the house.

Hours later, she was back on the ranch. It had been her sanctuary for years, the place that had protected her and insulated her from all the bad things in the world.

This ranch was still her home, it was where she was needed, but…she didn't need it to insulate her anymore. Dillon had pulled her out of herself. She'd thought things and said things and done things that wouldn't have been possible weeks earlier. She no longer needed the crutch of a place to hide away from the world. What she needed was the man she loved.

But his life was full, even more full than it had been when he had married Lisa. He had a major company to run that took up most of his time, a child to raise, social engagements. And those women in Chicago he'd meet weren't just novelty items. Some of them would know how to help him with his company. They would be more than convenient caretakers of his son. And they didn't have obligations in a state many miles away, Colleen thought, as she rubbed Mr. Peepers down, said hello to the rest of her animals and prepared to throw herself into running the ranch again.

This place and these tasks had always brought her forgetfulness before. Now, she hoped the ranch could help her get some perspective on Dillon and turn him into simply an unexpectedly nice memory.

But for the first time in her life, the ranch felt hollow. And there were no answers or comfort to be had here.

CHAPTER FIFTEEN

HE HAD let her go. Why had he let her go? Dillon was still asking himself that question days later.

But he knew the answer. All of his life, whenever he started getting too close to people, they backed away. And Colleen had done more than back away from him. She had all but run from him.

"She's just a person who's nice to everyone, Toby," he told his son. "We don't have an exclusive right to her, you know."

Toby was fussing with his fingers, chewing on his fist, looking generally unhappy and whimpering. The doctor had said he might be teething a bit early, but Dillon was sure that he missed Colleen.

"I'm still amazed that she confronted Lisa to keep her from taking you from me," he said. "It was a desperation move that required multiple lies, and our Colleen is not a liar. No matter how tough she tries to be, how much she tries to conceal things, the truth shows through in her eyes. See?"

he said, clicking through the photos of Colleen and him and Toby on the CD Millie had sent him with her thank-you note. "Look at her eyes when she's looking at you. She loves you, buddy, and I can't believe that Lisa didn't see that."

Toby started kicking and waving his arms when Colleen's face came on the screen. Maybe it was wrong to show him these pictures. He might think Colleen was really here.

But Dillon couldn't tear his eyes away. And when a photo of him and Colleen together appeared, when he saw the expression in Colleen's eyes as she turned to him…Dillon clicked through the photos again.

And again. And again, always coming back to that one. He looked into Colleen's pretty eyes. His heart began to pound. Then he turned to his child. "I know you're too young to understand, but you need to know this about your father. Every major decision I've ever made in my life since I've been an adult was based on logic. And only logic. I— I'm ashamed to say this, but I married your mother because I thought she'd make a good CEO's wife, I went overseas because I knew I could do some good, I went looking for you when I didn't even know if you were really mine, because…all right, that might not have been logic, but it didn't concern a woman, either. I don't lose my heart to women, Toby, and if I did, I'd ignore it. Logic tells me that following my heart ends up burning me every time. And being burned by Colleen would be much, much worse than being burned by any other woman. But…

"I just don't care much about logic right now. I'm running on total emotion. Feel free to throw this up in my face some day, son, but we're going to Montana. She might not want to see me. She might have taken up with that cowboy she kicked in the shins, the one who was falling all over her that night at Yvonne's. She might want me to leave, but…I have to risk it. This time I don't want to do the logical thing. I know she can't leave there. I know my business is here. But…heck, I don't know…at the very least we're going to see her one more time. No, I'm going to do more than that. Even if she asks me to leave, I'm going to do one thing. One totally illogical and crazy thing I've been thinking about.

"And yeah, I'm doing this eyes open. The truth is that I can feel heartbreak headed my way already, but I can't seem to back away. Let's lay the groundwork. And then, let's go find our cowgirl."

Colleen had just finished brushing the coat of Arianne, a pretty little black pony. She was washing the dust and dirt off herself when Harve drove up in his big Suburban with two other trucks following him.

Confused, Colleen tilted her head. Then, the passenger door opened, and her heart became a bass drum, thundering through her entire body. *Careful. Careful,* she told herself.

"Dillon, why on earth are you here?" she asked. "And Harve?"

"I'm just delivering him and the kid and all this stuff," Harve said, taking the baby from the big SUV and heading up to the house. The men from the other trucks started unloading lumber.

The two strangers didn't have to ask where it went. They already knew. Two weeks ago they had shown up, given Colleen a note from Dillon saying that by way of thanks he was building her bunkhouse for the ranch camp. And no, she didn't have any choice in the matter. He needed to do this.

She'd been grateful, but even sadder. Seeing something he was building for her and knowing she'd never see him again had sent her spirits plummeting.

But here he was. And she could barely breathe. "Dillon…" she began, but she didn't get any further. He pulled her right into his arms and kissed her. Hard. Then he kissed her again. Slowly.

"That will have to keep me satisfied for now," he said. "Even though it's not nearly enough."

"Are you…not staying?"

He stared at her, long and hard, his blue eyes bluer than water, bluer than her bluest bit of glass.

And hotter than…something so hot she couldn't think of a word. She just plain old couldn't think at all with him looking at her that way.

"I'm staying," he said. "All the forces of nature couldn't keep me from staying. Only you could make me leave. If you didn't want me here, I…"

"I want you here," she said, afraid of what he would say.

"I was prepared to beg."

Tears started to fill her eyes. She blinked them away. "Dillon…"

He shook his head. "I have something to do before I can talk."

Then he kissed her again and marched toward the lumber. He put on a tool belt, took his tools and began to construct a wall. He didn't look at her. He just worked, swinging his hammer, cutting the lumber, pounding the nails. He began to build her dream for her.

But hours later when he was still out there, she couldn't take it anymore. "Millie, give me some iced tea. The man is building my dream. The least I can do is bring him something to drink."

"Absolutely the least. Right, pumpkin?" Millie asked Toby, who was in his glory, surrounded and pampered by the women of the Applegate.

But for once Colleen didn't stop to listen to Toby. With glass in hand, she marched out to where Dillon worked. She moved right up next to him. He was shirtless. He was sweaty. She had never seen anything she wanted so much.

When she moved, he saw her there. "You shouldn't stand so close," he said, and she instantly felt chagrined. He wasn't feeling what she was feeling. "I didn't hear you coming. I might have accidentally hurt you, and that would kill me, Colleen."

"I was careful," she said, watching as he took his T-shirt and dried himself off. It was all she could do to keep from asking him if he would kiss her again. Her heart…hurt to be here with him, because the building seemed to be going up quickly. That comment about staying? He'd meant staying to build the bunkhouse, she knew. Soon, he would be gone again. How was she going to handle losing him twice?

She wasn't. She was going to be a total wreck, but he was doing this wonderful thing for her, and she hadn't even said one nice thing about it, hadn't even paid that much attention to the structure he was building with his own hands. And all for her. Colleen kicked herself for her insensitivity.

She handed him the tea. "May I look?" she asked, stepping up onto what would eventually become the threshold of the doorway.

He held up his hand and said, "Wait," but she had spotted something, and nothing was going to stop her now. She moved into the still roofless structure. The room was all golden wood, the scent of raw pine filling her nostrils, but what had drawn her inward was the wood itself. Sturdy and strong, the walls rose before her, the studs straight and precise. And on every stud, on every flat panel of wood, there was a message: Dillon Farraday loves Colleen Applegate; Dillon adores Colleen; You're the woman of my heart and always will be; You're my soul; With love, to the very best woman in Bright Creek.

"You weren't supposed to see all of this until I was done. These were just rough scribbles. I was trying to find the right words."

"The right ones?" she asked, dazed, her heart so full she couldn't think straight.

"I wanted it to be perfect. You—everyone takes you for granted. No one does or says what they should be doing or saying. The people of this town, your parents, that jerk of a guy who didn't know what he had when he had you…even me…we take and take from you and no one gives the right things.

"And you…Colleen, you forgive us. You even were forgiving Lisa. I could see that you were, and…that cowboy who treated you mean…you let him off with barely an apology. As for me…I let you go. I let you go when every cell in my body was screaming at me to beg you not to. I let you go because I was a coward, because I was afraid that you wouldn't love me back, but that shouldn't have mattered. I should have at least told you how much you mean to me, because you deserve to at least know that—"

He never got to say the words. Colleen launched herself against his bare chest, right against his heart. "You amazing, wonderful man. Did you think I wouldn't love you? I had to bite back tears all the way home so your pilot wouldn't tell you that I cried."

Dillon swore. "I made you cry?"

She shook her head vehemently. "*I* made me cry by falling in love with a man I couldn't have. I love you so much, Dillon, and I have for a long time."

He plunged his fingers into her hair, kissed her lips. "I was being so darn logical," he told her. "Not telling you I cared because I knew you didn't want to fall in love and I knew you were only with me because of Toby. I knew you couldn't care and had to be here, not with me."

"And *I* knew you had to be in Chicago, not with me."

He smiled against her hair. "It's a big, mobile world today. I can do a lot of work from a distance."

"And I have enough people working here and other friends in town willing to help that I don't have to be here all the time. The ranch isn't the same without you here, and I don't need to hide here anymore, but I would like to be here some of the time."

"As much as you need."

She rose on her toes and kissed him again.

"And this building, we'll paint over the words, of course," he said. "I want it to be your perfect dream bunkhouse for those girls from the city you want to help."

Colleen smiled up at him. "I don't want you to paint over the words. Maybe I'll get you to build me another one and I'll keep this one as a haven for you and me. I've got a great bed we can put in here and a new sofa sleeper some wonderful man bought for me."

"It better not have been Rob," he teased.

"Oh, this man's much better than Rob," she promised. "I've heard via the grapevine that the man that I'm talking about got his ex-wife to sign over custody to him, but he promised her that she would have visiting rights and she's even thinking of getting to know her little boy a bit. A man like that who puts his child's needs ahead of his own is a good man."

"You know you'll always be his real mother."

A tear slipped down Colleen's cheek. Dillon kissed it away. He got down on one knee.

"Dillon, get up," she said, tugging at him.

"No. I want this to be special. I want you to remember this day and I want to remember it, too.

Marry me, Colleen. Marry *us*, me and Toby. Be my wife. Be his mother. Be my love forever."

She took his carpenter's pencil and walked over to the wall. *I will,* she wrote. *I always will. I'll be your love forever. Be mine.*

"On this ranch, in the city, in the country, in a high-rise…everywhere. I'll love you always and everywhere." And he sealed his promise with another kiss.

"Even if I wear red cowgirl boots underneath my wedding dress?" she teased.

"Oh, I'm counting on that. I'm dreaming of it." He kissed her again and her heart turned to flame.

The sound of voices drifted to Colleen, and she and Dillon broke away and turned.

"What are you two doing?" Julie asked with a smile.

"I'm marrying Colleen," Dillon said.

"Harve, I know you've been around a lot lately, but now it's official," Colleen added. "The Applegate is no longer a no-men zone. Dillon changed all that."

"Good," Gretchen said, pulling out her camera. "Now if you two wouldn't mind kissing again, I want a picture to send out. Jace just e-mailed Millie. He and all your friends in Chicago want to know what's happening."

"What's happening is the best day of my life," Dillon said with a laugh.

"And much as we love all of you, Harve included, we'd like a little privacy right now," Colleen added. "No more pictures. And...close the door on your way out, will you?"

"We didn't see a thing," Millie said, closing an imaginary door. "You two just keep kissing."

So they did.

* * * * *

*Rancher Ramsey Westmoreland's temporary
cook is way too attractive for his liking.
Little does he know Chloe Burton came to his
ranch with another agenda entirely....*

That man across the street had to be, without a
doubt, the most handsome man she'd ever seen.

Chloe Burton's pulse beat rhythmically as he
stopped to talk to another man in front of a feed
store. He was tall, dark and every inch of sexy—from
his Stetson to the well-worn leather boots on his feet.
And from the way his jeans and Western shirt fit his
broad muscular shoulders, it was quite obvious he
had everything it took to separate the men from the
boys. The combination was enough to corrupt any
woman's mind and had her weakening even from a
distance. Her body felt flushed. It was hot. Unsettled.

Over the past year the only male who had gotten
her time and attention had been the e-mail. That
was simply pathetic, especially since now she was
practically drooling simply at the sight of a man.
Even his stance—both hands in his jeans pockets,
legs braced apart, was a pose she would carry to
her dreams.

And he was smiling, evidently enjoying the conversation being exchanged. He had dimples, incredibly sexy dimples in not one but both cheeks.

"What are you staring at, Clo?"

Chloe nearly jumped. She'd forgotten she had a lunch date. She glanced over the table at her best friend from college, Lucia Conyers.

"Take a look at that man across the street in the blue shirt, Lucia. Will he not be perfect for Denver's first issue of *Simply Irresistible* or what?" Chloe asked with so much excitement she almost couldn't stand it.

She was the owner of *Simply Irresistible*, a magazine for today's up-and-coming woman. Their once-a-year Irresistible Man cover, which highlighted a man the magazine felt deserved the honor, had increased sales enough for Chloe to open a Denver office.

When Lucia didn't say anything but kept staring, Chloe's smile widened. "Well?"

Lucia glanced across the booth at her. "Since you asked, I'll tell you what I see. One of the Westmorelands—Ramsey Westmoreland. And yes, he'd be perfect for the cover, but he won't do it."

Chloe raised a brow. "He'd get paid for his services, of course."

Lucia laughed and shook her head. "Getting paid won't be the issue, Clo—Ramsey is one of the wealthiest sheep ranchers in this part of Colorado. But everyone knows what a private person he is. Trust me—he won't do it."

Chloe couldn't help but smile. The man was the epitome of what she was looking for in a magazine cover and she was determined that whatever it took, he would be it.

"Umm, I don't like that look on your face, Chloe. I've seen it before and know exactly what it means."

She watched as Ramsey Westmoreland entered the store with a swagger that made her almost breathless. She *would* be seeing him again.

Look for Silhouette Desire's
HOT WESTMORELAND NIGHTS
by Brenda Jackson,
available March 9 wherever books are sold.

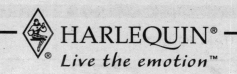

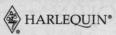

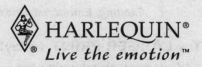

HARLEQUIN®
INTRIGUE®

BREATHTAKING ROMANTIC SUSPENSE

Shared dangers and passions lead to electrifying
romance and heart-stopping suspense!

Every month, you'll meet six new heroes
who are guaranteed to make your spine tingle
and your pulse pound. With them you'll enter
into the exciting world of Harlequin Intrigue—
where your life is on the line
and so is your heart!

THAT'S INTRIGUE—
ROMANTIC SUSPENSE
AT ITS BEST!

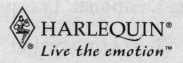

HARLEQUIN®
Live the emotion™

www.eHarlequin.com

INTDIR06

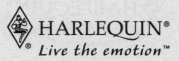

Harlequin® Historical
Historical Romantic Adventure!

*Imagine a time of chivalrous
knights and unconventional ladies,
roguish rakes and impetuous
heiresses, rugged cowboys
and spirited frontierswomen—
these rich and vivid tales will
capture your imagination!*

*Harlequin Historical . . .
they're too good to miss!*

HHDIR06

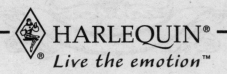